THE SEA STAR BAKERY

A WILLA BAY NOVEL

NICOLE ELLIS

LEAPING RABBIT PRESS

1

Cassie

Cassie pulled up to the Inn at Willa Bay, the brakes on her ten-year-old minivan squealing as she brought it to a stop. *Better add that to the list*, she thought. Since the divorce, it seemed like something broke every time she turned around. At this rate, her bank account would soon be depleted.

She stepped outside and shut the car door slowly, taking in the view. The sun was already high in the sky on this beautiful June morning, its rays bouncing off the glittery blue waters of Willa Bay. A soft breeze fluttered the skirt of the sleeveless lavender dress she'd chosen to wear to church that day.

The front door of the Inn opened about six inches. "I'll be out in a minute, dear," Celia James called out. "I just need to feed the dog." Celia's little white terrier, Pebbles, flashed in and out of view as he jumped around behind his mistress.

Cassie grinned. Her ex-husband, Kyle, had wanted a

golden retriever, but she'd vetoed that long ago knowing she'd have ninety-nine percent of the responsibility for a pet. She'd never been a dog person, but there was something about Pebbles's antics that always brought a smile to her face. "Take your time," she shouted back at Celia. There were definitely worse places to be stuck waiting for someone.

Cassie regarded the Inn. Her good friends, Zoe and Meg, along with Shawn – Celia's grandson and Zoe's new boyfriend – had recently purchased a half-interest in the dilapidated old resort from Celia and had grandiose plans for renovating it. While Meg had chosen to keep her job for a while longer at the Willa Bay Lodge where she, Cassie, and Zoe had all worked, Zoe had quit her job as the Lodge's event coordinator soon after purchasing the property.

They had only been working on it for about six weeks, but their efforts had already made a difference. With the help of Shawn's experience in carpentry and remodeling old houses, they'd replaced all of the rotten siding and repainted the exterior a charming shade of blue that matched the waters of the bay. The lawn had recently been clipped short, and roses bloomed below the wraparound porch, perfuming the air with their scent. When Cassie had been here last week with her ex-husband, their son, Jace, and daughter, Amanda, to celebrate Jace's birthday at the beach, it looked like some work had been done on the old gazebo as well. Things were really coming along.

The front door swung open and Celia's walker peeked out, drawing Cassie's attention away from the renovations – just in time to see a streak of white dart past Celia and down the stairs. "Pebbles! Get back here!" Celia slowly rolled the walker out onto the porch.

Pebbles stopped on the bottom step and turned around to eye his mistress, his tongue lolling from his mouth. He yipped at Celia once, then turned back to the yard, his eyes lighting up as he sensed freedom. Celia sighed. "Pebbles, get back here. I'll have Shawn take you for another walk this afternoon, I promise."

Cassie jogged forward as fast as she could go in her one-inch heels and grabbed Pebbles's collar before he could get any further. Celia had assured her before that he didn't usually venture very far away when he did get out, but Cassie wasn't taking any chances.

"Gotcha," she said to the little dog as she picked him up. He wriggled in her arms, but didn't fight too hard to escape.

Celia waited on the porch, wearing a calf-length floral dress with cap sleeves. Her snow-white hair was wound into a bun on the back of her head and chunky clip-on earrings adorned her earlobes. She stepped aside to let Cassie take Pebbles back in. "I swear that dog thinks he's a greyhound or something."

Cassie laughed and set Pebbles well inside the entry hall, hurrying to close the door securely behind her before he could follow. Celia locked the door and then made her way to the side of the porch, where Shawn had installed a long ramp for her and future guests with mobility issues.

Cassie got Celia settled into the car, then sat down in the driver's seat, tucking her flouncy skirt under her legs. She drove away from the Inn and down the long gravel driveway, which used to be littered with potholes that made her worry about her minivan's suspension, but had been one of the first things Zoe and Shawn had repaired when they'd taken over ownership of the property.

At the end of the driveway, Celia leaned over, grinning

like the Cheshire Cat. "I have amazing news for you!" She fidgeted in her seat, unable to contain herself.

Cassie often gave Celia a ride on Sundays to the local Lutheran church they both attended. On weekends, when Cassie's ex had the kids and it was just her and Celia in the car, it gave her a chance to get to know the older lady better. Normally, Celia was very even-tempered, so this level of excitement from her was unusual.

Cassie lifted her eyebrows, but maintained her attention on the road as she turned onto Willa Bay Drive. "What is it?"

The words bubbled out of Celia's mouth. "Edgar Johnson is moving to Arizona."

"Okay?" Edgar Johnson was in his late seventies, and it was general knowledge that his wife hated the rainy weather in Western Washington, so this wasn't exactly earth-shattering news.

"He's shutting down the bakery and leasing out the space." Celia's fixed her eyes on Cassie's face.

"That's too bad. I always liked Edgar's Bakery. His scones are delicious." Cassie turned onto Main Street and then made a quick right to head up the hill to where First Lutheran Church perched high over the town.

Celia sighed loudly as Cassie parked the car. She put her hand on Cassie's arm. "*You* should lease the bakery space from him."

Cassie snorted. "I can't afford my own bakery. I just need a small catering kitchen to work in." She'd been decorating cakes on the side for years while working at the Willa Bay Lodge as their pastry chef. Up until a couple of months ago, they'd let her use the kitchen for her side business. That is, until the owner's daughter, Lara, came back to town with cake decorating aspirations of her own. Cassie had been lucky enough to find a temporary solution in Meg's mother's catering kitchen, but with the busy summer event season now in full swing, it was becoming difficult to share the space.

"I already told him you were interested." Celia sat back in her seat, regarding Cassie with a smug grin.

Cassie's eyes grew so wide that she thought they might actually pop loose. "You did what?" Celia may have been outspoken and stubborn, and her heart full of good intentions, but this stunt took the cake – literally. "I'm not ready to open up my own shop."

Celia shrugged. "You'll never truly be ready. Sometimes you just have to jump when life presents you with an opportunity you can't pass up."

"But I have to pass it up. I barely have enough money as it is." An image of her two kids flashed through Cassie's mind. Jace had ADHD and was recently diagnosed with autism, so she'd been researching programs that might help him be more successful in school. Even with her side job, funds were tight.

"Didn't you have an appointment with the Small Business Administration last week?" Celia asked.

Cassie brushed her hands over the top of her head and through her shoulder-length blonde hair, the familiar motion soothing her. She had given some thought over the past few weeks to opening her own bakery, but the SBA had crushed that dream. "Yeah, and they basically confirmed that this isn't the right time for me to open up my own business." Without savings, the start-up costs would kill her, and even if the bank would approve it, she wasn't going to risk putting her house up as collateral for a business loan.

"Well, I still think it's a good idea." Celia put her hand on the door handle. "The location is excellent, and you'd have a built-in clientele."

Cassie closed her eyes for a moment, then opened them to meet Celia's gaze. "I'll consider it." She knew opening her own bakery wasn't a possibility for her right now, but Celia looked so happy that Cassie didn't want to stomp on her joy. She got out of the car and retrieved Celia's walker from the trunk before coming around to open the passenger-side door.

Cassie helped Celia out of the car, and they walked into church together, neither of them speaking of the bakery lease again. As they entered the building, a woman in her sixties, with curly hair and a huge smile, approached them. "Hey, Cassie," she said.

"Hi, Betty," Cassie replied.

Betty then wrapped an arm around Celia's shoulders and addressed the older woman. "How are you doing, honey? It's so good to see you. I've been visiting family in Texas and just heard about your accident."

Celia grinned. "I'm doing well. A hip fracture isn't going to keep me down."

Betty beamed at her. "I'm glad to hear that. We need you here." She moved her hand to rest on Celia's, which was clutching the walker. "Mary Lou and I were just discussing a fundraiser for the library. Are you interested in helping with it?"

"That sounds wonderful," Celia said. "After the last levy failed, the library can use all the help it can get."

"No kidding." Betty frowned. "We're hoping to raise money for them to update their current collections, and maybe even renovate the sitting areas." She tilted her head in Mary Lou's direction. "Do you want to chat with us for a bit before the service begins?"

Celia glanced at Cassie. "Do you mind?"

Cassie shook her head. "Not at all. I was hoping to grab a cup of coffee first anyway. That cup I had this morning didn't seem to do much." It was an excuse, but she knew it was important for Celia to feel needed, and the library fundraiser was perfect for her.

They met back up before the church service, and sat together a few rows from the front. Cassie found her mind wandering as the pastor sermonized. Celia's news about Edgar's Bakery closing had given Cassie a lot to think about. It wasn't the right time for her to open a bakery of her own, but for a moment she let herself imagine what it would be like. Jace had given her the perfect name for a bakery in Willa Bay: The Sea Star Bakery. She loved his analogy about how she was regenerating her life after the divorce, just like a sea star could regrow its limbs.

Until lately, Cassie would have said she was content in her job at the Lodge, but having Lara Camden back in town was making her miserable. Lara had taken over the kitchen in the mornings for the cake decorating business she'd started on the side, essentially stealing Cassie's baking facility. But Lara's father, George, owned the Lodge and let her do whatever she wanted. Cassie grimaced. Beside her, Celia must have noticed the sour look on Cassie's face, because she nudged Cassie gently with an imploring look in her eyes.

Cassie focused on Celia, giving her a small grin, then returned her attention to the pastor, who was speaking about "loving thy neighbor" – an apt sermon considering Cassie's recent musings about Lara. A tiny bit of guilt flared in Cassie's chest, but she tamped it down. She would try to be nicer to Lara, but that didn't mean she had to like her.

After partaking in the refreshments hour after church, Cassie drove Celia home and walked her to the door. As they neared the top of the ramp, she caught a glimpse of Zoe and Shawn, who were sitting on the far side of the porch, gazing out at the bay while eating sandwiches and drinking tall glasses of what looked like iced tea.

Zoe stuck her head around the corner. "Hello! I thought I heard you pull up. Do either of you want to join us for lunch? Shawn made plenty of tuna fish salad for sandwiches."

A deep voice announced from behind her, "With extra pickles!"

Zoe shook her head. "Shawn and his pickles." She zeroed in on Cassie and Celia. "Are you interested?"

Cassie smiled. "No, I'm having lunch with Kyle and the kids. We're trying to do more things together as a family, for the kids' sake."

Celia covered her mouth and yawned. "Thanks, Zoe, but I'm beat. I plan to take a long nap."

"We'll be sure to be quiet for you then." Zoe waved. "See you both later. Have fun at lunch, Cassie." She disappeared back around the corner.

Celia entered the house, pausing in the entryway while blocking Pebbles with her foot. "Promise me you'll think about the bakery?"

Cassie sighed. She should have known Celia wouldn't give up so easily. "Yes. I'll think about it."

Celia nodded curtly. "Good. I think it would be a wonderful opportunity for you. I'll make sure to let Edgar know you're interested." She smiled sweetly at Cassie and shut the door.

Cassie's mouth gaped open, but then she couldn't help but laugh at the elderly woman's moxie. When Cassie was eighty-something, she'd be lucky to have half Celia's spirit.

～

Cassie left the Inn, driving home to change quickly into jeans and a red tank top before meeting Kyle and the kids at Pizza Kingdom. The pizzeria's parking lot was almost full when she arrived, probably due to the after-church crowd. When she got inside, she scanned the packed restaurant for her family and smiled when she saw them. Kyle had managed to snag a prime table near the arcade.

"Mom's here," Kyle announced when she got close.

"Hey, Mom." Amanda jumped up from the table. "Dad said we could go to the arcade once you got here."

"Can I get a hug first? I haven't seen you guys in two days." Cassie held her arms out, and her daughter leaned in, allowing her mother to hug her. While they were embracing, Jace slid out of the booth. Cassie released Amanda and wrapped her arm around her son, giving him a quick squeeze. "Okay, okay. You can go play now. Did Dad give you money?" She glanced at Kyle, who nodded.

"I ordered pizzas already, too, because they're slammed here today." He turned to the kids, "Have fun, but come back in about twenty minutes. The pizzas should be here by then." Jace and Amanda were off to the arcade before he'd even finished his words. Kyle turned back to Cassie. "Man, I wish it were this easy to entertain them in my little apartment." He frowned. "It's fine when it's just me, but they're bouncing off the walls when three of us are in it."

She laughed. "Don't worry, they're like that at home too."

"Really?" He eyed her with disbelief. "I don't remember it being like that."

"That's because you were never home." Her words came out sharper than she'd intended. He winced visibly and took a long drink from his soda. She gave him an apologetic smile. "I'm sorry. I didn't mean it like that." After two years of divorce and mild animosity toward each other, they'd reached a truce a few months ago. She'd promised herself she'd try to be kinder to him in the future and not hold old grudges against him.

"You did mean it like that." His eyes were sad. "But you're right, I wasn't home enough when the kids were younger." He picked up his napkin, nervously rubbing his hand against the rough edges. "I'm trying to do better now."

She took a deep breath. "I know you are. It's okay." There had never been any major issue that had led to their divorce, like financial or marital infidelities – it had been death by a thousand little cuts. They'd been high school sweethearts and married right after college. Maybe they'd married too young. All she knew was that as Kyle moved up the ranks at his accounting firm and she stayed home to take care of the kids, his late nights at the office had come between them, and they'd grown apart.

The waitress came by with two steaming pans of pizza and set them on metal stands already at the table.

"Thanks," Kyle said, before the waitress scurried away. He slid a slice of the combination pizza onto his plate. "Should we go get the kids?"

Cassie took a piece of the same pie, reaching to sever the string of cheese connecting her plate to the pizza pan. The aroma of warm mozzarella, spicy pepperoni, and herbed marinara sauce permeated the air, but she knew she'd burn her mouth if she tried to bite into it immediately. "Nah, let them play for a while longer. The pizza needs to cool a bit anyway."

"Remember when we were first married and could barely afford a cheese pizza from here?" Kyle's eyes clouded over. "We'd splurge on a small pizza, take it home, then throw the couch cushions on the floor and watch movies together all night.

A wave of nostalgia washed over her. They'd had a lot of good times together. "I remember." She swallowed a lump in her throat. What she wouldn't give to go back in time and fix everything that had gone wrong between them. But all of that was water under the bridge now.

Kyle sensed her discomfort. "So, what's new with you? How did that meeting with the Small Business Administration go? I haven't talked with you since then."

She hunched her shoulders and stared off toward the kids. "It wasn't great. Basically, they said they'd help me figure out how to start a business, but when it got down to it, I chickened out. I can't risk the house on a lark like this."

Kyle sighed. "It's not a lark. You're an amazing baker."

"Thanks. But, unfortunately, that's not enough. I'm just going to have to keep looking for a cheap space to rent where I can make my cakes." She dabbed the corner of her napkin at a drop of marinara sauce that had landed on the vinyl, red-and-white checkered tablecloth. Should she tell him about Edgar's Bakery? Part of her wanted to share Celia's news, but another part knew he'd try to talk her into leasing the space, and she didn't want to deal with that.

"What about Edgar's Bakery?" he asked. "I heard Edgar is looking for someone to take over the bakery space. That would be perfect for you."

She stared at him. Did everyone in town know about Edgar and his wife moving to Arizona? "How did you know about that?"

He chuckled. "Willa Bay's a small town. Edgar's a client of mine, and he asked if I knew anyone who might be interested in the building."

It was like everyone was conspiring against her and her conservative financial sensibilities. "I can't afford it." She was starting to sound like a broken record. She bit into the pizza to test the temperature. If she had something in her mouth, she couldn't be forced into this discussion. The hot marinara sauce blistered her tongue, and she dropped the pizza on her plate.

Kyle rested his arms on the table and leaned toward her. "If it's only about the money, I'm happy to help you as much as I can. I'm up for a promotion at work." The earnest expression on his face tugged at Cassie's heartstrings. *Get it together, Cass. You don't want to borrow money from Kyle.* She'd worked too hard since the divorce to make a life of her own and didn't want to go back to being dependent on him again.

She eked out a smile. "Thanks for being so supportive about this. If this opportunity had come up in a few years, I'd be all over it, but now isn't the right time."

"Right time for what?" Amanda asked from behind her. Jace pushed past his sister and slid across the booth, grabbing a slice of pepperoni pizza in one fell swoop. Amanda peered at her mother.

"It's not the right time to start a business now." Cassie gave Kyle a look that implored him not to argue with her.

"Oh, that again," Amanda said. "I thought you already had a cake decorating business anyway." Kyle scooted over on the bench seat, and Amanda sat down next to him, daintily setting a piece of pizza on her plate.

Cassie smiled at Amanda. "I do. And that's all I need for right now. I'm busy enough with just that and my regular job."

"Thank goodness." Amanda took a small bite, then swallowed before saying, "We just saw my friend Kaci in the arcade. She's here with her mom and her mom's boyfriend." She made a face. "I hope you don't have any time to date. That would be, like, so weird!"

Cassie nearly sputtered out the water she'd just sipped, and her cheeks flamed. "I don't have plans to date anytime soon."

Her eyes darted to Kyle, who was watching her intently. Neither of them had really dated since the divorce, at least not that she knew of, so they'd managed to avoid having the "introducing the kids to a significant other" conversation. Now, she found herself wondering if Kyle had started dating – not that it mattered to her. Her stomach ached as though she'd been stabbed in the gut.

She turned to Amanda and said in a steely voice, "I'm enjoying my independence right now and discovering what *I* want out of life. I don't intend to get involved with anyone for a long time – not that you or your brother have a say in whether or not I date."

Amanda shrank back against the booth, and Cassie cringed. Next to Cassie, Jace was happily chowing down on pizza and had seemingly missed the whole exchange. Kyle opened his mouth as if to say something, then snapped it shut.

Cassie sighed. "I'm sorry, honey. It's been a long day."

"That's okay, Mom." Amanda smiled at her and gestured to the pizza. "Have some food. I think you're getting hangry."

Normally, Cassie would have reprimanded her for the pre-teen snark, but this time, Amanda had a point. Cassie picked up her pizza. "You know, I think you may be right."

She took a huge bite filled with gooey cheese, and they all followed Jace's lead in demolishing the pies. Cassie did her best to stay cheery the rest of the afternoon, but inwardly she struggled with the conflicting emotions she experienced around Kyle and the joy that consumed her in the brief moments where she allowed herself to imagine her own bakery.

What she'd said to Amanda had been true – she'd never expected to be a divorced mom of two at the age of thirty-two, and she was still trying to discover what she wanted to do when she grew up. She'd had so many dreams for her future with Kyle, but the divorce had brought many changes to her life, some good and some bad. One thing was for sure though: leasing Edgar's bakery space was not in the cards for her.

2

Zoe

Zoe collapsed into a chair on the porch of the Inn at Willa Bay, clutching her project checklist like a lifeline. In truth, it *was* a lifeline. There was so much to do to get the Inn ready for guests that without her notebook, she'd be lost. June was already nearly half-over, and the days were passing faster than she'd like.

"You okay?" Shawn asked from behind her.

She turned to see him holding out a glass of iced tea. "More or less." She accepted the glass from him, drinking half of it in one long gulp.

"More? Or less?" He sat down next to her in a cushioned chair and searched her face. "You've got to slow down, or you're going to burn out."

She set the tea down on a side table. "I can't. We have to keep to the schedule if we want to be ready by the end of August."

He sighed deeply. "It will all work out."

She wished she had his confidence. He may think her

to-do list was causing her stress, but it was the only thing keeping her sane. She knew if they stuck to it, they could get everything done in time.

"What's on the agenda for today?" he asked, glancing up at the sky. "Looks like a good day to get some outdoor stuff done."

"I hope so. The roofers are coming today." A minor pang of irritation shot through her. She'd already reminded him about the appointment about a million times. He'd vetted and hired the roofing company, but she'd scheduled them. Fixing the holes in the Inn's roof was one of the first things that she, Shawn, and their co-owner, Meg, had wanted to accomplish when they'd bought the property at the end of April, but every company in town had been booked until now. Shawn had installed a few temporary patches so they could do some basic repairs on the upstairs guest rooms, but they wouldn't hold much longer.

"That's today?" He shrugged. "I guess I'll be managing that then."

She forced a smile. "Uh-huh. I'd kind of hoped you would. I don't know much about roofing." She consulted her list. "While they're working on the upstairs, I'm going to finalize our plans for the kitchen remodel."

Although they'd put most areas of the property that guests wouldn't see on the back burner for now, they weren't sure the kitchen would pass county health regulations in its current state. They weren't planning on serving meals out of the Inn's kitchen – that would come later when they renovated the barn into a full-service restaurant. However, they did need a place to make coffee and prepare store-bought pastries in the morning, and they wanted to have the option to expand their offerings in the future. Meg had been off work from her job as sous-chef at the Willa Bay Lodge on Monday and Tuesday, so she'd come over to help select the materials and plan the layout. Her experience with kitchens and insights into the most efficient layouts had proven invaluable.

While Zoe had quit her job at the Lodge almost immediately upon buying the Inn, Meg had chosen to keep her job until they were able to focus on the restaurant phase of their renovations, so most of the organization and management of the multitude of projects at the Inn had fallen on Zoe. Shawn helped as much as possible, but his time was taken up with the day-to-day maintenance and supervising their contract workers. Meg helped when she could, but Zoe wished she had someone to help with the bigger projects.

Zoe took a deep breath of fresh air and let the sparkling waters of Willa Bay calm her. Everything was going to be fine. The roofers were coming today, and everything was proceeding on schedule. She pushed herself up out of the chair, laced her fingers together, and stretched them out in front of her for a moment, releasing some of the tension in her shoulders.

Shawn stood as well. He reached forward and grabbed her around the waist, drawing her to him. She resisted at first because there was so much to do, but then let herself lean against him and rest her cheek on his chest.

"It'll all be okay," he whispered into her hair, his hands pressing into her back reassuringly.

Zoe nodded imperceptibly, trying to soak up some of his optimism. Having a partner to shoulder some of the responsibility was taking some getting used to, but she was grateful to have him in her life.

She would have happily stayed in his embrace for hours, but there was so much to do. Reluctantly, she stepped back, gazing into his dark blue eyes. "Thank you – for the tea and for everything else."

He tipped his head to her. "You're very welcome." He cleared his throat. "I'm going to check on a few things before the roofers arrive." He gave her a quick peck on the lips. "I'll see you a little later. Try not to stress too much."

She nodded. "I'll try."

Shawn strode off out of sight, and Zoe surveyed the grounds. Things were definitely shaping up around here. Her gaze paused on the old gazebo. As much as she wanted to save the old structure, Shawn had informed her it would need to be completely rebuilt. Years of neglect had resulted in rotting beams and sagging floors. Still, it retained some of its original charm and Zoe couldn't wait until they could return it to its original condition from when the Inn first opened in the early 1900s.

Once upon a time, the Inn at Willa Bay had been the premier resort in town, with the large guest house anchoring the property and twenty cottages stretching along the shoreline. Tourists used to flock to the area from Seattle and surrounding communities until air travel had become commonplace. Since the downfall of the resort industry, Willa Bay had reinvented itself as the wedding capital of the Northwest, but the Inn had never quite regained its original popularity. When Celia's husband died, she hadn't been able to keep up with maintenance, and the whole place had fallen into disrepair. Zoe had been renting one of the little cottages on the property for a decade. Now she was excited to have the opportunity to share the Inn's beauty with all of their future guests.

Zoe took a final look out at the bay, then walked inside to work on the kitchen. When she entered, Celia waved at her from the living room. "Good morning, Zoe," she called out.

Zoe smiled and walked into the living room. "Hey, Celia." Next to Celia, Pebbles barked and wagged his tail. "And you too, Pebbles." He barked again.

"So, what's on the agenda for today?" Celia asked from the couch.

"The roof is finally getting fixed," Zoe said. "And I'm going to finish up the plans for the kitchen so they can get started on the remodel next Monday. We'll move the microwave and coffee pot in here and set up a hot plate so you can still cook. If you need an oven, feel free to use mine in my cottage."

Celia nodded. "I don't use the oven much anymore, but you never know when you'll want fresh-baked cookies." She grinned. "Do you know how long the remodel will take?"

"I'm hoping it will only take a week or two," Zoe said. "It depends on whether they find substantial damage to the walls or need to replace any of the floorboards."

"Sounds about right." Celia looked at her surroundings. "Do you know when you'll do the living room?"

Zoe consulted her plans. "After the kitchen is done. I don't want to spread anyone too thin, and we didn't want to make things more difficult for you than they have to be."

After Celia's accident a couple of months ago, she'd been living in a rehabilitation center for a while. During that time, Zoe and Shawn had remodeled her bedroom so that part of the renovation would be complete before she moved back in.

"Thanks," Celia said. "It's a little rough living in a construction zone, but I appreciate everything you've done with the place." She shook her head. "I never could have managed any of this, let alone afforded it."

"Well, we're glad to see the Inn getting prettied up too." Zoe nodded to the kitchen. "Anyway, I'd better get going. Maybe we can take a coffee break together later."

"That would be great." Celia beamed at her while petting Pebbles. "See you later."

Zoe walked down the hallway to the kitchen, stopping in front of the entry to take it all in with a critical eye. A new sink would be installed in the same location under the window, but almost everything else in the kitchen would be moved. She and Meg had decided on a cheery color scheme in blue and white that would evoke thoughts of the bay outside, and the floors would be laid with durable, water-resistant vinyl plank that closely resembled real hardwood.

She was making a few notes to the kitchen contractor about how to arrange the backsplash tiles when she caught a glimpse of the round clock on the wall. Time had flown by. It was almost eleven, and she hadn't yet heard from the roofers. She went to the front door and checked the driveway, but it was empty. She returned to the kitchen and sat down at the table to dial the roofing company's office.

"Ralph's Roofing," a cheerful female voice sang out.

"Yes, hi. I'm calling from the Inn at Willa Bay. We were supposed to have our roof replacement started today, but nobody has arrived yet." She tapped her pen against her notebook.

"Hmm. Let me check and see what's going on." The woman was silent for about a minute, then came back on the line. "It looks like they're running way behind on their other job. It's one of those big apartment complexes they're building in Everett."

"Okay ..." Zoe said slowly. "So, what does that mean for us?"

"I'm so sorry, but it looks like we'll need to reschedule you."

A pit formed in Zoe's stomach. "Reschedule to when?"

"Hmm. Does late August work?" the woman asked. "We shouldn't get too much rain this summer anyway."

"Late August?" Her plans hinged on getting the roof done this week. It was taking all Zoe had to not scream at the woman, but she kept her tone professional. "That's not going to work for us. We're supposed to open the Inn to the public in late August."

"I'm sorry, ma'am. That's the best I can do." The woman didn't sound terribly sorry.

They may just be a random client to the roofing company, but this was critical to Zoe. "There's nothing you can do to get us in sooner?"

"We can see if there's a cancellation, but other than that, no." The woman paused, then asked, "Did you want me to book you into the late August slot?"

Zoe gritted her teeth. "Sure."

"Fantastic." The woman's voice was about one hundred times more upbeat than Zoe felt. "We'll call you in August to let you know when we'll be there."

Zoe hung up the phone, not knowing if she should have told the woman off, or have been grateful that they were at least on the roofing company's calendar.

"Hey, I was thinking about grabbing some lunch," Shawn said as he walked into the kitchen. "Are you hungry?"

"Not really." Her numbness was turning to anger. "The roofing company isn't coming."

"What?" He came over to the table and sat down. "Why'd they cancel?"

She shrugged. "Something about a big job running over."

"Oh, no." He frowned. "One of the older online reviews of their company said something about them being flakey, but the more recent reviews were positive. I thought maybe it was just a case of bad management a few years ago."

"You hired them knowing they could be flakey?" The pitch to her voice rose. "We needed them to be here this week."

Contrition filled Shawn's face. "I thought it would be okay. I'm sorry, Zoe. I'll start calling other companies."

Zoe's cheeks grew hot with anger. "Yeah. And this time, make sure they're reliable." She got up from the table and stalked out of the room. Behind her, Shawn sighed, but she didn't stop until she was outside, descending the stairs to the beach.

The railing beneath her hand was smooth, and the stairs were new and stable. They were one of the first things at the Inn that Shawn had taken care of when he'd come to Willa Bay. He was always trying to make things better for her and Celia, and she knew she shouldn't have blown up at him. It hadn't been his fault, but in the heat of the moment, he'd been an easy target.

The beach stretched out in front of her, and her breathing evened out as the waves and soft ground underneath her sneakers eased her stress. She wouldn't go so far as to say that her cares were washed away, but a walk on the beach always made things seem better. She strolled along the pebbled sand for fifteen minutes before turning around to return to the Inn – and to apologize to Shawn for her outburst.

3

Meg

Meg Briggs rubbed her eyes, willing the blurry order form to come into focus on the computer screen in her boss's office. She had to get this right because last week she'd made an error on the meat delivery and they'd ended up with an overstock of chicken breasts. They'd frozen the chicken, but if there was an issue this time, the vegetables would be a lot harder to preserve for later.

She'd been up late last night working at the Lodge, then had gone over to the Inn that morning to help Zoe with some last-minute changes to the kitchen renovation plans. There had been too many of these long days in the last month, and now she was paying the price.

"You okay?" her boss, Taylor Argo, asked. While she'd been caught in a daze, he'd seemingly materialized across from her like a ghost.

Meg jumped, causing the desk chair to lurch backward in an unsettling manner. Well, now she was fully awake. "I'm fine, just a little tired."

He grabbed a stack of books off his desk and moved them to a bookshelf in the corner of the room, then peered at her closely. "Were you out at the Inn this morning? You look like you could use more sleep."

She forced a smile. "I'll be okay once I have another cup of coffee." She didn't want to complain too much because her boss had been incredibly understanding about the situation. He knew she'd bought a resort with her friends and would be leaving her position at the Lodge in a few months to open up a restaurant that would directly compete with his. He'd acted happy for her and assured her that her job at the Lodge was available for her for as long as she wanted it.

"Hmm …" He stared at her with skepticism. "How about you go get that coffee now."

She pointed at the computer screen. "It'll only take a few more minutes, I promise. I want to get this complete before I start the dinner prep."

"Okay, but let me know if you need help. I'm worried about you." Taylor took a final look at her, then exited the room, his long white chef's jacket swinging behind him, and his spiky black hair barely clearing the top of the doorframe.

Meg finished the vegetable order for the weekend and submitted it online to their produce vendor. She got up from the desk and yawned loudly. Now it was definitely time for that cup of coffee, or she wouldn't make it through the rest of the evening.

Taylor was cooking something on the range but turned and smiled at her as she walked past. In the main part of the kitchen, her friend Cassie was carefully lifting sugar cookies in the shape of butterflies off a baking sheet and placing them on a wire rack to cool.

"Hey," Cassie said, without taking her eyes off the task. "I'm almost done here. Want to take a break with me?"

"Definitely." For Meg, the best thing about working at the Lodge having her two good friends working there with her. Now that Zoe had quit, it was only Cassie left. It still seemed odd that she wouldn't see Zoe zooming around the Lodge as she effortlessly juggled multiple events at the same time. "I was going to pour myself a cup of coffee. Want one?"

"Sure." Cassie walked over to the dish sink with the empty tray. "A few of the cookies didn't turn out quite right, so we can have them as treats." She removed a container of light-yellow frosting from the refrigerator and brought it over to her worktable.

Meg settled at the other end of the counter with two mugs of coffee, perching atop a tall barstool. Cassie quickly frosted two of the butterfly cookies that had lost a portion of their wings and slid them onto plates before joining Meg. "You look awful," Cassie said.

Meg was just about to bite into her cookie, but stopped and set it down on the plate. "I know. I feel awful. There's just not enough time in the day to work here and at the Inn. I feel so bad leaving it all to Zoe and Shawn, though. I need to do my share."

"Didn't the three of you decide that it would be best for you to keep your job until it was time to turn the barn into a restaurant?" Cassie reminded her.

"Yeah, but I didn't think I'd feel this guilty about letting them do all the work." She took a big bite of the buttery sugar cookie, her teeth sinking into the soft frosting. The infusion of caffeine and sugar was making her feel better, but she knew it would be short-lived. Something had to give. "Do you ever wish you'd taken Celia up on her offer to buy into the Inn too?" Meg asked.

Cassie wiped a few crumbs from her mouth with a paper napkin. "No. I know it's a great opportunity, but I don't think it's the right one for me at the moment. I mean, everyone's been bugging me about taking the lease on Edgar's Bakery, and I don't even think I could make that work. I'm kind of in a weird place with everything going on at home and my cake decorating business. I don't want to rock the boat with a huge business endeavor."

Taylor came into the kitchen, followed by a man pushing a dolly stacked high with boxes. He led the man to the walk-in refrigerator, then came over to where Meg and Cassie were talking.

He sighed, then asked in a formal tone, "Meg, when you're done, can I please have a word with you?"

Meg almost choked on her cookie. She'd never heard Taylor so somber. "Uh, sure. I'll be there in a minute."

"I don't mean to rush you, it's not an emergency." Taylor shifted in his blue converse sneakers.

Meg and Cassie exchanged glances.

"We're almost done here." Cassie stood and gathered their crumb-strewn plates.

Taylor nodded. "I'll be in my office."

Meg stared down at her coffee, then up at Cassie. "What do you think that's all about?" Her stomach clenched. Very little fazed Taylor, but his expression had been so serious. Was he having second thoughts about her working at the Lodge?

"I don't know." Cassie shrugged. "I'm sure it's nothing, though. Taylor loves you." She smirked. "Literally."

Meg glared at her. "This isn't the time, Cass. He actually looked upset."

Cassie was fond of the idea that Taylor had a crush on Meg. Once in a while, he did something that made her wonder if Cassie was right, but she usually brushed off her friend's romantic notions.

"Well, good luck," Cassie said. "I'm going to finish frosting these cookies and then head home, but let me know what Taylor says."

"I will." Meg took a deep breath, walked to Taylor's office door, and rapped on it sharply.

"Come in," he said.

Meg opened the door and stood there awkwardly, something she hadn't done since her first day at the Lodge when she'd had newbie jitters. "Hey. You wanted to see me?"

His face was drawn as he gestured for her to sit down across from him. When she was seated, he said, "I hate having to have this conversation with you, but I thought you should know." She held her breath as he picked up a stack of dinner menus. "The menus you printed out for tonight are from a month ago."

She stared at the menus he held out. Sure enough, the date at the top was May. "I'm so sorry. I must have printed the wrong ones." She shook her head. "It won't happen again."

He smiled at her softly. "I know you didn't mean to, but this isn't the first error you've made in the last few weeks – there have been several mistakes with customer entrées and an issue with the meat order last week." He leaned across the desk at her. "Between the Inn and your work here, you're exhausted and off your game. I'm worried about you." Kindness and caring radiated from his eyes, and she breathed a sigh of relief. He wasn't going to fire her.

"I'm sorry." She didn't know what else to say. At this point, quitting the Lodge didn't seem like a viable option, and she couldn't shirk her duties at the Inn either.

He sighed. "It's okay. I just wanted to make you aware of it and let you know that I'm here for you if you need me." He peered at her. "I know the Inn is important to you, but when you're here at the Lodge, I need you at your best."

She nodded. "I understand."

"If you need help, let me know," he said, his gaze still focused on her.

"Okay. I definitely will. Thank you again for telling me about the menus." She pushed back and blindly stood from her chair, her brain numb. How was she going to make all of this work? She softly closed Taylor's office door and walked back out into the kitchen.

Cassie was leaning against the wall, facing away from Meg as she peeked around the corner. "Cassie, what's wrong?" Meg asked.

Cassie held a finger to her lips. "Shh." She motioned for Meg to follow her a few feet, then pointed wordlessly at the partially cracked open door of the walk-in refrigerator.

Meg cocked her head to the side. "Uh ... I didn't leave that open."

Cassie sighed. "Lara's here to get a cake out of the cooler, and she's full of 'good' news about her plans to lease the bakery space from Edgar. I think she just wanted to rub it in that she's getting her own bakery."

"Oh." Meg frowned. "I thought you didn't want to start your own place right now. Do you?"

Cassie bit her lip, and her eyes glistened. "I don't know. It's a pipe dream. I would have loved to lease the bakery, but I simply can't afford it." She cast another glance at the refrigerator door. "It seems like Lara always gets what she wants." A tear beaded in the corner of her eye, and she swiped it away with the back of her hand. "I know it's irrational, but I can't help thinking that life is so unfair. I've worked hard to build my cake decorating business in Willa Bay, and Lara just swoops back to town and immediately comes out on top."

"Ah." Meg eyed her thoughtfully. "Could you still lease the space if you wanted to?"

"I don't know." Cassie's looked down at her shoes. "It sounds like she has it pretty wrapped up."

As if on cue, Lara exited the refrigerator with a rolling cart in tow. A tall cake sat atop the cart. Precise bands of forest green lace had been piped onto a bottom base of snow-white fondant. Little silver flowers were artfully arranged around each tier. However Meg and Cassie might feel about Lara, she did have talent.

"Hi, Meg," Lara said. "Nice to see you again."

Meg nodded and forced out a nicety. "Your cake is beautiful."

Lara beamed. "I know." She eyed Cassie, tilted her chin up, and turned back to Meg. "This is for one of the biggest weddings of the year that's happening tomorrow. For some reason, they wanted to get the cake a day early."

"Ah." Meg wasn't sure what to say. She didn't want to further inflate Lara's ego or to upset Cassie, who looked like she was fighting hard to keep from saying something nasty to Lara. "Well, I'm sure it will be a beautiful wedding."

"It will." Lara shut the refrigerator door. "It'll be nice to have my own place soon. I assume you've heard I plan to lease Edgar's old bakery space?"

"Uh-huh," Meg said.

Lara wrinkled her nose. "It's going to take a lot of work to make that place presentable, but it'll do."

Cassie clenched her hands into fists, and Meg

searched for a change of subject. "Do you need help getting the cake out to your car?"

"I'm fine. I have a custom van to transport the cakes." Lara checked the clock on the wall. "I'd better get moving, though. I have a new client to meet after I drop off this cake at the wedding venue." She threw a smug look at Cassie, who shifted her gaze to the floor.

When Lara was out of the room, Cassie crumpled against the wall. "I really hate her." She sighed. "I know I tell my kids not to say 'hate' but it seems to fit how I feel about Lara Camden."

Meg loathed seeing her friend so miserable. "I'm sorry. If it makes you feel better, I think I saw a small flaw in the back of the cake."

Cassie's face brightened. "Thanks. That does help a little." Her face turned cloudy again. "But it doesn't help with the long-term implications of all of this. If Lara leases the bakery, she'll have room to expand her cake decorating business, whereas I'm about to lose my space in your mom's commercial kitchen. There just isn't enough capacity for both their catering business and my cakes. I don't want to go back to using the Lodge's kitchen because I can't rely on it being available."

"So, lease the bakery." Meg shrugged. "If you feel that strongly about it, beat Lara at her own game."

"I can't." Cassie straightened and strode forward a few steps. "I'll just have to figure something else out." She flashed a smile at Meg. "Thanks for being such a good friend and hating Lara along with me."

Meg grinned at her. "That's not too big a hardship."

"I'm heading home now," Cassie said. "I'll see you tomorrow, okay?"

"See you later," Meg answered. After Cassie left the kitchen, Meg realized that she'd never told her friend why

Taylor had called her into his office. With how Cassie was feeling, though, it was probably for the best. She didn't want to add any other worries to Cassie's already full plate.

Meg got to work on preparing produce for the evening's entrées, taking even more care than normal to make sure everything was cut precisely. Taylor had been very understanding about her recent mistakes, but she didn't want to give him any more reasons to find fault with her performance, or to make him feel conflicted between his roles as both her friend and her boss.

4

Kyle

"Knock, knock." Kyle looked up from his computer to see Dana Timonds in his open office doorway, her red manicured fingernails bright against the light wood of the frame. Unlike many of the younger employees at the CPA firm, she'd never taken to casual Fridays and was wearing some kind of black jumper-type dress with a red blazer over it.

He looked up from his computer and smiled at her. "Come in." He and Dana had worked together for over ten years, both coming to Johnson & Associates as accounting majors fresh out of college. They'd always been competitive as they earned their CPA licenses and worked their way up in the firm, but had remained friends through it all.

She came over to his desk, the spikes on her high heels catching on the thin pile carpet with every step. She pulled out the chair across from him and slid into it.

"Promotions are coming up next week. Have you heard anything yet?"

He shook his head. "Nope. You?" Their firm always issued promotions after the spring tax season, and this year both he and Dana were up for senior manager positions.

She shook her head, then leaned across the desk. "I heard Andrew was being offered a shareholder position."

"Seriously?" Kyle asked. "He's only been a senior manager for a year."

She shrugged. "It's all about who you know and kiss up to, I guess." She glanced at the silver watch on her wrist. "I have a client meeting in a few minutes, but I'll catch you for happy hour tonight, right?"

He smiled. "Yep. I'll be there." Now that he didn't have Cassie and the kids to come home to at the end of a long day, he'd found himself hanging out more often with the single crowd at work. It wasn't that he necessarily liked going out with them, but it was better than the alternative of returning to an empty apartment at the end of the work day.

After Dana left his office, Kyle shot a furtive glance at his office door, then opened the top drawer of his desk. He looked down at the framed photo he kept in there of Cassie, the kids, and him out at the beach. His mom had taken the photo about two years before the divorce, back when things between him and Cassie were good. He kept school photos of Jace and Amanda on his desk, but after he and Cassie split up, it felt weird to keep this picture out in the open. He'd thought of taking it home, but he couldn't bring himself to get rid of it.

He focused on Cassie's cheerful smile. She'd always had a way of making family events so much fun for everyone. He missed that. Although they'd recently made an effort to do more as a family, it was bittersweet, because it made memories of happier times between the two of them seem not so distant. At the pizza parlor, however, Cassie had made it quite clear that she didn't need a man in her life, especially him. Her comment about not wanting to be dependent on anyone for a while had stung. He closed his eyes for a moment, then opened them and slid the drawer shut.

When she'd announced that she wanted a divorce, it had seemed to come out of nowhere. To be fair, they'd attended a few couples counseling sessions, and while she didn't seem as happy as she used to be, he'd thought everything was still fine between them. Maybe not like it had been before, but change was a normal part of marriage, right?

He'd been so focused on building his career as a tax accountant that he hadn't paid enough attention to what Cassie needed. He hadn't noticed her becoming more distant or expressing interest in pursuing a career in cake decorating, although she claimed she'd told him several times.

He pushed his chair back from his desk and ran his fingers through his hair. Apparently, there had been a lot of things he hadn't noticed, both with Cassie and with their kids. He intended to change that, though. It was too late to save his marriage, but he could still make an effort to be there for his kids.

He glanced out the frosted glass wall in his office as blurry shapes made their way down the hallway. Did he even want the promotion? It was the next natural progression in his career, but it would mean an increase in hours and possibly more travel. Thinking about the partners at the firm, a few were happily married, but a greater percentage were older men on their second or third families. His stomach lurched. When he and Cassie were first married, he could never have predicted that they'd eventually divorce. He'd already made the mistake of letting this job come before his family in the past – would a promotion make things even worse?

He looked at the small photos of the kids. Jace had recently been diagnosed with autism, and Cassie wanted to get him into some of the therapies the nurse practitioner had recommended. Their insurance would cover part of it, but not all. Amanda was getting older and was asking for gymnastics lessons. Judging by their crooked teeth, both kids would need braces soon. He needed the money this promotion could offer.

Kyle's desk phone rang and he picked it up. "Hello?"

"Call from Mr. Andreas," announced the receptionist in a chirpy voice. "He wants to talk to you about quarterly taxes."

"Thanks, Natalie." Kyle answered the call from his client, happy to have a distraction from his internal debate. At this point in his career, he could do most tax planning in his sleep, but this at least provided something other than his personal problems to think about.

At four thirty he wrapped up his work for the day and put on his jacket. A few of his co-workers, including Dana, were already waiting in the lobby.

"Hey," he said as he joined Dana and another one of the tax managers.

"Hey." She beamed at him, flashing a row of straight, white teeth. "I think we're just waiting for John." She looked past Kyle and smiled at a short man who'd just walked in. "Looks like he's ready. Let's go."

They filed out of the offices, which were located on the top floor of a three-story building in what was known as the business district of Willa Bay. Essentially, this area was about a block wide and contained all of the taller buildings in town, although none were over four stories high. Happy hour was usually at O'Reilly's, an Irish pub down the street.

In the pub, they crowded into a few tables and ordered drinks and appetizers. As he sipped the dark chocolate porter he'd ordered, he chatted with some of his colleagues. Everyone wanted to talk about the upcoming promotions, but thinking about being promoted made his head spin. Toward the end of happy hour, his co-workers left one by one to go home to their families or their extracurricular activities.

When only Dana and he remained, she got up and moved down the line of empty tables to sit across from him.

"How's it going?" she asked, sliding her glass of wine onto the table.

He gave her a tired nod. "Fine."

"You look a little off tonight." She tipped her head. "Is everything okay?"

He sighed. "Yeah. It's just been a long day. That, and all I have waiting for me at home is another beer." He held up the beer he'd been nursing and smiled at her. "Are you heading out soon?"

She grinned. "I don't know. I was thinking about it, but maybe I'll stay a while. You look like you could use some company." She flagged down the waiter and ordered a basket of hot wings for them to share.

He eyed her. "Don't you always go to a yoga class or something on Fridays?"

She shrugged. "It's Pilates, but I can skip it. I'd rather hang out with you."

He sipped his beer. "Well, thank you, I guess." He wasn't sure whether he was grateful to have the company or depressed that she was taking pity on him for not having something more exciting to do on a Friday night.

"Well, you don't have to sound so excited about spending time with me." She grinned to show she was teasing him.

"I *am* glad you're here."

The wings arrived, and he grabbed a piece of celery and dipped it in the small cup of blue cheese dressing. They chatted for another hour, and Kyle found himself enjoying the evening. He and Cassie used to have a cup of coffee after the kids went to bed and chat about everything under the sun – that is, before everything went haywire in their relationship. Talking with Dana wasn't quite the same, but it was nice to have another adult to talk to outside of work.

After they'd had a basket of French fries, another round of wings, and split the check, Dana stretched her arms out. "I'd better get home because I've got an early morning yoga class tomorrow." She touched her flat stomach and laughed. "After pigging out tonight, I'd better not skip it."

"Sounds like a fun class." He couldn't imagine anything less fun than waking up early on a Saturday morning to exercise, but to each their own.

"Oh, it is." Her whole face lit up. "There's something invigorating about being up before everyone else on a Saturday. It starts my whole weekend off on the right foot."

"Well, I'll let you to it." He hopped off his barstool and stretched his legs. They'd been sitting there chatting for longer than he'd realized. "Have a nice weekend."

Dana nodded. "Thanks." She hesitated for a moment. "I had a great time with you tonight. Do you think you might want to do this again? Just the two of us?"

His breath caught, and he blinked a few times. She was asking him on a date. "Sure." He smiled at her. "I'd like that."

"Great." She flashed him a toothy grin. "Let's talk about it next week. I think it would be fun."

"I do too." He almost choked on the words. Although he didn't dislike the idea of going on a date with her, this was a new step he hadn't anticipated. "See you Monday."

"See you." She smiled at him again, then picked up her purse and exited the bar.

Kyle waited a few minutes longer, then walked out to his car. He hadn't given much thought to dating anyone, much less Dana, but the idea intrigued him. Unless he wanted to go home to an empty apartment for the rest of his life, it was about time to take a step toward his future.

5

Cassie

"So, where did you want to go first?" Cassie stopped at the end of Celia's long driveway and flipped her turn signal on to head toward town. "You said you needed groceries and had a few other errands to take care of, right?" It was supposed to be Cassie's weekend with the kids, but Kyle had taken them to a special Minecraft exhibit at a museum in Seattle for the day. When Celia had asked for a ride to the grocery store, Cassie had been happy to help.

Celia nodded. "I'd like to stop off at Edgar's Bakery first, though. I've been craving one of his famous cinnamon rolls, and you know how fast they sell out of them on the weekends. Plus, with the nice weather, the tourists will be out in full force today."

Cassie's stomach grumbled on cue, and she laughed out loud. She could almost taste the delicious spread Edgar used to coat his cinnamon rolls. It was a cross between cream cheese frosting and buttercream icing that she'd never quite been able to replicate. Maybe now that he was getting out of the business, he'd be willing to share his recipe.

"Sounds like a plan." She followed Willa Bay Drive for about a mile, then took a right onto Main Street, slowing considerably as she drove through town. Celia had been right to worry. At ten o'clock in the morning, many of the shops were just opening, but there were already hundreds of tourists and locals milling around the sidewalks and ambling over the crosswalks.

Edgar's Bakery was on the far end of Main Street, on the side opposite the river. In this area of Willa Bay's downtown, the buildings were all attached to each other and had been designed in the Mediterranean revival style that had risen to popularity in the early 1900s. The bakery sported a yellow-and-white striped awning and wrought iron tables and chairs in front for patrons who wanted to eat their pastries outside. At the moment, they all were full. A dog sat under one of the tables, its tongue hanging out as it observed all of the commotion around them.

A wave of sadness swept over Cassie. Edgar's was a big part of the community and would leave a gaping hole in the social fabric of Willa Bay when it closed. She'd grown up going to Edgar's every weekend as a child – it had been a post-church tradition for her family. Her favorite choice had been the shortbread cookies that were cut into seasonal shapes and decorated with a thick layer of multi-colored frosting. She'd passed the love for those cookies on to her own kids, and they'd all miss the delicious treats. Perhaps Lara, or whoever became the next owner of the bakery space, would offer cookies as well, but they wouldn't be quite the same. Cassie may not be fond of Lara, but at least under her ownership, the space would remain a bakery and not be converted into another gift shop.

Cassie found a handicapped parking space around the corner from the bakery, hung up Celia's parking tag on the rearview mirror so she wouldn't get a ticket, and helped the elderly woman out of the car.

"It's such a gorgeous day." Celia admired the clear blue sky with her rheumy eyes, then grinned at Cassie. "I have a feeling it's going to be a good day too."

Cassie laughed. "I admire your positivity." She'd woken up that morning feeling a similar sense of well-being, perhaps due to the bright sunshine seeping through her open blinds, or in anticipation of a day off work without the kids. She and Celia walked slowly down the sidewalk to the bakery, sidestepping the large dog lounging next to its owner's chair.

Inside, a group of people waited patiently for their turn. A little kid had his nose smushed up against the glass case, staring at the cookies with eyes as big as saucers. Two employees were helping customers, and Edgar himself was in the middle of assisting someone. Celia waved at him when they entered, and he flashed her a grin to acknowledge their presence.

The shop smelled amazing, with the aromas of warm baked bread, fresh fruit fillings in the Danishes, and, of course, the strong scent of cinnamon. Cassie and Celia stood off to the side, near the few tables by the window. The bakery wasn't huge, but during non-busy times, it was a great place to hang out with friends and enjoy a cup of brewed coffee and a pastry. Cassie craned her neck to peer around the other customers, and let her eyes rove over the baked goods.

She paused on the half-dozen or so cinnamon rolls remaining on a white paper doily. "Looks like there's a few left if the people in front of us don't take them first."

"I'm sure it will be fine," Celia said calmly.

Cassie was still trying to figure out what she planned to order, when Edgar made his way through the crowd to them. He was pleasantly plump, a side-effect from years of bakery ownership, and wore a flour-specked, royal-blue apron over a T-shirt and faded blue jeans. When Cassie was young, Edgar had worn his brown hair cropped close to his head. Now, a few wisps of gray hair formed a circle at the top of his pink scalp.

He wrapped his arm around Celia and squeezed her shoulders gently. "How are you feeling?"

"I'm doing well," she replied. "My hip is almost healed, and seeing the improvements at the Inn is giving me a new lease on life." A far-off look came into her eyes. "I can't wait to see it brought back to its former glory."

He nodded. "I know what you mean. I'm a little worried to see what happens with my bakery after we move to Arizona, but life is full of changes, right?"

"Right." Celia beamed at Cassie, which Cassie found odd. "Speaking of the bakery, is now a good time to talk?"

He chuckled. "As good as ever, I guess." He gestured to them. "C'mon back to my office. I've got those cinnamon rolls you wanted boxed up for you."

Cassie had a sinking feeling as she followed Celia and Edgar into the back of the bakery. Celia had told her she wanted to get there early so she could get cinnamon rolls, but it sounded like Edgar was expecting her. Something about this situation was fishy.

They walked through the brightly lit main production room of the bakery and into a small enclosed office sandwiched into a back corner, across from a large supply closet.

"Have a seat," Edgar said, motioning to the two chairs across the desk from the one he was settling into.

Cassie hesitated, not sure why they needed to sit to pick up some cinnamon rolls.

Celia lowered herself into the nearest chair, then tugged on Cassie's arm. "Have a seat, dear."

Cassie sat next to Celia, her body tense.

"So, I hear you're a wonderful baker," Edgar said to Cassie.

Cassie looked over at Celia, then blushed. "I hope I am. I love doing it."

Celia shook her head. "She's being too modest. She's the best baker I've ever met – excluding you of course." Edgar smiled, and Celia continued. "Her cakes are absolutely flawless."

Cassie smiled slightly. "Thank you, Celia." Her brain was going a hundred miles an hour. This felt like a job interview, which was odd because Edgar planned to sell his business soon. Even if she was looking for another job, surely he wasn't in the market to hire anyone.

Edgar's steel-gray eyes bored into her face. "Are you interested in leasing the bakery from me when I move? Of course, you're free to make any changes you'd like."

Cassie's heart hammered in her chest. Lease the bakery? Of course she was interested, but her capability to do so was a different matter.

"Um ..."

"She's interested," Celia said firmly.

Cassie shot her a questioning look. "I am?"

"Of course you are." Celia sighed. "Stop being afraid to go after what you want."

Edgar's gaze moved between them as they spoke. "Cassie, is this something you want to do?"

"Well, yes, but I can't afford it right now. With the house and the kids, I'm already stretched too thin." It made Cassie ill to say that out loud to Edgar. She was so close to grabbing what she wanted, but finances were holding her back.

"I'll give you the seed money for the bakery," Celia said. "You can lease the space from Edgar and do some remodeling to make the place your own. When you're wildly successful, you can pay me back."

Cassie's eyes misted over. Celia really was a kind woman. "You're assuming I'll be successful. What if I never earn enough to pay you back?"

"Oh, you will." Celia folded her hands in her lap. "I have faith in you. You just need to have some faith in yourself."

Edgar slid a piece of paper toward Cassie, which contained the essential lease terms. She reviewed them, sucking in her breath at the monthly cost. It was more than she'd expected, but she'd probably been vastly underestimating the cost of leasing a building on Willa Bay's Main Street.

After he'd given her a few minutes, he asked, "So what do you think?"

Cassie hesitated, and Celia patted her arm. "Cassie?" she prompted.

A mixture of fear and hope welled up in Cassie's chest. "I think I want to do it."

Edgar gave her a huge smile. "I'm happy to hear that. I think you're going to be just the right person to take over for me. Willa Bay needs this bakery, but I wasn't sure I'd find the right fit."

Something occurred to Cassie. "What about Lara Camden? I heard she was going to lease the space."

Edgar shrugged. "I gave her some information about the bakery lease, but that was about it. We hadn't talked about it yet." He cocked his head to the side. "Besides, something about her rubs me the wrong way. I'm not sure I would have wanted to give up my bakery to her."

Cassie fought to contain a smirk. Lara did have that effect on people.

"So, what do we do next?" Cassie asked, looking around the small office as the realization dawned on her that this would soon be *her* office. Her stomach rolled, and she felt a little like throwing up. This was a huge undertaking, and she'd just agreed to it on a whim.

Kindness emanated from Edgar's eyes, as if he understood her anxiety. "I'll get the paperwork, and you and Celia can sign it." He stood and turned around to access a beige filing cabinet behind his desk, rifling through the folders. He plucked out a few sheets of paper that were stapled together, and set them on the desk before sitting down again. He turned them toward Cassie. "I need you to fill out your information at the top, then we'll go over the terms again before you and Celia sign."

She nodded, almost in a daze, wondering what had just happened. She'd come in for cinnamon rolls, and maybe if she was feeling extravagant, a few iced cookies to take home to the kids. Now, she'd be walking out as the owner of a bakery.

Celia squeezed her arm. "This is good for you, I promise."

Cassie nodded. She'd needed to find a new space to rent to make her cakes, and a bakery of her own *had* always been her dream, but this had come up faster and sooner than she would have liked. Still, maybe this was what she needed. She picked up a ballpoint pen from the desk and with trembling fingers, filled out her name, address, and other information.

When she was done, Edgar went over the lease terms with them again, and both Cassie and Celia signed on the lines he indicated. After everything was complete, he made copies of the lease agreement and handed one to each of the women.

"I'm closing down my operations in a week, so that's when your lease will start." His eyes clouded and he sighed, looking slightly miserable. "I've been here for thirty years. I can't believe this is the end."

Celia leaned over and rested her hand near his. "I'm sure you and Betsy will enjoy Sedona, though. Think of all the golf you'll get to play."

He brightened. "I know. It's just going to be a huge adjustment after having the bakery be such a big part of my life for so long." He laughed. "What am I going to do at four o'clock in the morning now that I don't need to come in to bake?"

Celia laughed. "Sleep, perhaps?"

He stood from his chair. "I *am* looking forward to sleeping in once in a while. But speaking of work, I'd better get back out there. Saturday mornings are crazy."

Cassie's head buzzed as she exited the building, clutching the lease agreement in her hand. Celia had stuck the box of cinnamon rolls and her own copy of the lease in the basket of her walker and didn't look shell-shocked in the least. Then again, this had all been Celia's doing, so it wouldn't have been a surprise to her like it had been for Cassie.

I came in for cinnamon rolls and left with a lease, Cassie thought. What was Kyle going to say about that? She paused, causing Celia to bump into her. She and Kyle were divorced – she didn't need to tell him about the bakery. So why was he the first person she wanted to tell the news to?

When they were back in the car, Cassie took Celia to the grocery store, the library, and then back home.

"Thank you, dear," Celia said as Cassie set her groceries on the kitchen counter. "I really owe you one for all of your help today."

Cassie stared at her. "You helped me lease a bakery. I'm pretty sure I'm the one who owes you."

Celia shrugged. "Eh. It was the least I could do for you. And you deserve a chance to go after your dream. I have all this money from selling half of the Inn, and not much to spend it on. I couldn't think of a better place to invest it in than you and your bakery. I'm sure it's going to be a huge success."

Cassie sniffled a little and leaned forward to give Celia a huge hug. "Thank you," she whispered into the older woman's ear. "Thank you so much for believing in me." She straightened. Now, it was time for Cassie to believe in herself.

6

Libby

The luggage and camping supplies piled high in their driveway was making Libby's head spin. How had they accumulated so much stuff, and more importantly, how were they going to get it all in their minivan without leaving one of the kids at home?

"Mommy! Can I bring Olaf?" her older daughter, Beth, asked, holding up her stuffed snowman.

Libby shook her head. "Uh-uh. You already chose a stuffie to bring with you. If we take anything else with us, your brother is going to need to stay home."

Beth grinned. "Really? Camping might be more fun without him."

Libby sighed. "No. Not really. Now go put Olaf in your room and come back here to help me with packing."

Beth cocked her head to the side. "Why can't Daddy help you?"

Libby gritted her teeth. "I don't know where Daddy is."

Gabe had been out late again last night and then disappeared earlier that morning. They were supposed to leave an hour ago, but without the help of another adult, she'd fallen behind on the schedule. Her head pounded, both from lack of sleep and from the stress of wrangling the belongings of six people for a weekend of camping.

"I'll go find him." Beth skipped away before Libby could tell her that Gabe's car was gone, leaving her Olaf doll in the driveway.

Libby picked him up and set him on the bench on the front porch before returning to the car. Gabe was much better at packing the van than she was, but at this point she didn't really have a choice but to start on the job. She picked up the heavy, eight-person tent she'd purchased that week and slid it onto the floor of the back seat, along with the blow-up mattresses and everyone's sleeping bags. The kids in the back row were just going to have to deal with having stuff under their feet.

The other supplies looked more manageable now, but something was missing. She groaned. The ice chest. She'd forgotten to bring out the massive white cooler from the kitchen. That was going to take up half of the trunk.

After lugging the ice chest outside and stowing it away, she shoved the rest of their stuff into the minivan, barely fitting the last item in under the ceiling. She checked her watch. It had taken her an hour, and Gabe still wasn't home.

She plucked her cell phone out of her pocket and dialed her husband. It rang once and went to voicemail. She stared at it. He'd sent her directly to voicemail. What was going on? Lately, Gabe had been increasingly distant with her and the kids, but she'd hoped a family vacation would remind him how lucky they were to be a family.

A minute later, he returned her call with a text: *Be home in ten minutes.*

And that was it. No excuse, no reason why he wasn't home to help. Libby slammed the liftgate down and leaned against the car, tears brimming in her eyes. This wasn't how life was supposed to be. She and Gabe had both wanted a big family, and they'd made the decision together to have her stay home with the kids. In more recent years, she'd gone back to work part-time with her mother in their catering business. But still, she hadn't signed on to be alone all the time with the kids.

When Gabe pulled into the driveway ten minutes later, Libby had corralled three of the four kids in the entry hall and was having them each use the bathroom, then put on their shoes. She saw Gabe walking up the sidewalk, his phone glued to his ear, and she fought hard to stay calm.

He nodded as he rushed past her and up the stairs to their bedroom. She counted to five, then ushered the kids out to the minivan and shouted at her oldest child, William, that it was time to go. William came thundering down the stairs.

"Are we ready to go?" he asked. "Dad's still upstairs."

"I know." She forced a smile. "He'll be down in a minute. Get out to the minivan, and try to keep your siblings from killing each other."

William rolled his eyes at her. "Like they listen to me."

"Do your best," she said firmly.

William went outside, and she heard him shouting to his brothers and sisters like a drill sergeant. She left the mess behind and went upstairs, where Gabe was pacing the floor of their bedroom, talking rapidly to someone. She stood there, not speaking, and he held up a finger to let her know he was busy. Libby went into the bathroom and splashed some water on her sweaty face, then came back into the room. Gabe was grabbing his cell phone cord and a few other things and tossing them into a small bag.

"I don't know that cell phones are even going to work out there," she said.

His eyes bugged out. "Seriously? Are we going to the middle of nowhere?"

She shrugged. "It's a state park. The cell service is supposed to be spotty."

He huffed and zipped the bag with an exaggerated movement. "This is going to be a long weekend." He clopped down the stairs and out the door.

Libby took a moment to compose herself, catching her reflection in the floor-length mirror next to the dresser. Her face was flushed with the exertion of packing the car and getting the kids ready, and her long dark hair hung in sweaty tendrils. She bit her lip, trying to hold back tears. Taking a deep breath, she grabbed a hair tie off the dresser and wound her hair up into a messy bun. For her kids' sake, she wanted this camping trip to go well. With school, work, and extra-curricular obligations, the family rarely had time to spend together. The kids were getting older faster than she'd like, and she wanted to make some special memories with them while they were young.

The kids were in various stages of getting their seatbelts on, and Gabe had the car running when she slid into the passenger's seat.

"So where is this place?" Gabe asked.

"It's in the Cascades." Libby entered the name of the state park into her phone and turned on the GPS navigation system.

For the next few hours, Libby and Gabe barely spoke as she played referee between the kids in the back of the van. By the time they'd reached their campground, her nerves were frazzled, and she was already wondering why she'd thought camping with four kids and a grouchy husband was a good idea.

After checking in and getting their tent set up at the campsite, she released the kids to go play on the playground. "William, make sure you watch Kaya. Don't let her out of your sight."

"Aye-aye, captain." He saluted her and ambled off with the other kids in the direction of the playground.

Libby sat down at the picnic table to rest. "I need some caffeine after that."

Gabe retrieved his phone from the car and slammed the driver's side door shut. "You're the one who wanted to do this."

She flinched. "I thought you wanted to take a family vacation too. This seemed like the perfect time, right after school was out and before all of the kids' summer activities start."

He stared at his phone screen and swore. "I missed a call."

She took a shuddering breath and fixed her eyes on him. "Doesn't work know you're on vacation?"

He sighed. "I work in sales. I'm never on vacation. Besides, how do you think we're paying for this trip? I can't just ignore my customers."

Libby caught a note of worry in his voice. Was this why he'd been so standoffish lately? She badly wanted to believe that he was acting like this because of work, and not because there was another woman in the picture. "Is there something going on at work? Anything I should know about?"

He slid his finger along the phone's screen and looked up at her. "No. Everything is fine."

She'd believe that when her kids became perfect little angels. Something was up, but whatever it was, he didn't have any intention of sharing it with her. "Do you want to take a walk along the lake with me?" she asked. It had been so long since they'd spent any quality time together, just the two of them.

"No." He held his phone up in the air, assessing the cellular signal strength. "I need to get to a location with better cell phone reception so I can call this guy back."

"Can it wait until tomorrow?"

"No, Libby, it can't. I have to make money for our family when I can." He looked over at their new tent and then back at her. "You're always spending money so irresponsibly. Like this tent you bought without even talking to me about it first." A vein on his neck twitched and his fingernails were white against the black plastic of his cell phone case.

She reared her head back as though she'd been burned. In all their years of marriage, they'd rarely fought about money, and she was well-known in her family for her thrifty nature. She'd spent days researching tents and comparing prices in stores and online. The tent she'd selected should last them a long time, and she'd even purchased it at a huge discount sale. "We needed a tent that could fit all of us. There was no way we could squeeze all of our sleeping bags into the one we used years ago." He had to know she wouldn't have bought the tent unless it was absolutely necessary. Where was this reaction coming from?

He moved away from her and gazed up at the blue sky to gather his thoughts, then turned back around. "I don't want to fight about this right now. I need to take this call, and maybe when I come back we can go on that walk, okay?"

He stalked off toward the entrance to the campground, waving his phone slowly in the air like a divining rod as he searched for bars of service. Libby got up from the table and walked behind their campsite to a thicket of trees, then sat down on a log to think. Growing up, she and her sisters had spent a lot of time in nature, and it always helped her to get away from everything to work through whatever was bothering her.

She idly ran her fingers over a patch of fuzzy green moss and let her heart rate settle. Gabe had been acting oddly for months, but he wouldn't admit to anything being amiss. They'd always been a team, and it stabbed her heart every time he shot down her efforts to communicate. She'd never have imagined her husband having an affair, but did anyone really expect that kind of thing? Was he planning on leaving her?

She gazed up at the leafy branches high above her and focused on a squirrel jumping from tree to tree. She really wanted to talk to one of her sisters, but they'd both been so busy lately.

Normally, Libby would confide in her youngest sister, Samantha, but she'd been distant for a while. Libby had chalked it up to it being the end of the school year and Samantha having a lot to do as she transitioned from being a teacher into her summer jobs. Libby had recently worked through her relationship issues with her other sister, Meg, and although they were now on good terms, Meg was overwhelmed with work and her responsibilities at the Inn at Willa Bay. But, sheesh, Libby really missed talking to them. And worries about her husband being unfaithful definitely wasn't something she wanted to share with her mother.

Even with seeing family all the time and constantly having her kids around, Libby felt more alone now than she'd ever been in her life. Part of her was scared to find out what was going on with her husband, but she needed to know the truth, whether it be good or bad. After over a decade of marriage, he owed her that much.

7

Meg

Meg sat back in her seat at the Wedding Belles Café and kicked her feet up on the chair opposite her. She sipped her almond-flavored latté and gazed out the window at the river flowing below the deck. At this time of year the water lapped high against the riverbank, teeming with snow runoff from the mountains. By August, the water levels would be considerably lower, although still navigable by boat in the dredged channel.

She rotated her ankles and wiggled her feet, trying to keep them from freezing up. She'd helped Shawn paint the walls and ceiling of the main stairwell at the Inn that morning, and had stood at an awkward angle for most of that time. But he and Zoe had been so excited to show her the progress in the kitchen, so it had been worth going out there before work.

However, it had been a little disappointing for her. Zoe was consumed by all of her projects at the Inn, and Cassie had surprised everyone by announcing her intention to open her own bakery. Even with her role as part-owner, Meg's restaurant at the Inn at Willa Bay wouldn't open for at least a few more months, and that was if all the renovations went according to plan. Meg's life would resemble a virtual Groundhog Day – going from the Inn to the Lodge and then to sleep, every day the same.

Over her shoulder, a man cleared his throat. "Do you mind if I sit with you?" He held a ceramic mug in one hand while he used the other to gesture to the chair where her feet were resting. "Every other seat in the café is occupied, and it looks so nice and sunny out here."

"Oh. Sure." Her face flushed as she whipped her feet off the chair. "Sorry. I was just resting my legs for a minute."

"No problem." He set his cup down on the table, pulled the chair out, then settled down in it. He stretched his arm out to her and smiled disarmingly. "I'm Theo."

She shook his hand. "I'm Meg. Nice to meet you, Theo." She took a closer look at him. He was about her age, with a cute smile, disheveled sandy-blond hair and a carefree air about him.

He drank from his mug, then set it back down on the table. "Are you from around here?"

She laughed. This was starting to feel like a pick-up, rather than a simple need for an unoccupied chair. "I am local, yes. Are you?"

He grinned. "I'm local for now, but we'll see where the wind takes me – literally." He chuckled a little. "I live aboard my sailboat. It's moored down at the marina right now."

"Really?" Meg lifted her eyebrows. "You live on your boat?"

"Yep. Been doing it for over three years now. I work in online marketing, so I'm free to go anywhere I can get a signal to get on the Internet." He looked toward the marina. "I've been living in the southern part of Puget Sound for a while, but I decided that it was time to mix it up this summer with a trip up north."

She nodded, intrigued by his nomadic lifestyle. If she weren't so close to her family, the idea of working remotely and traveling wherever she felt like would be awfully appealing. "How do you like Willa Bay?"

He shrugged. "I'm not sure yet. I've only been here since last night. From what I've seen, though, it's beautiful." He frowned. "There's an awful lot of wedding-themed shops and restaurants, though. What's that about?"

She laughed. "We're known as the Wedding Capital of the Northwest. Between that and the tulips fields, Willa Bay thrives on tourist traffic."

"Hmm. I'm not usually big on tourist towns, but I'd love to be proven wrong." He looked into her eyes, and she squirmed inwardly at his directness. "Would you be interested in showing me around town? Maybe dinner tonight?" He glanced at her left hand. "That is if you're not a newlywed yourself."

Meg was in the middle of sipping her latté and snorted a little at his comment, splashing milk onto her face. Theo looked at her with amusement as she dabbed her cheeks with a napkin. When she'd recovered, she said, "No. Definitely not married. Not even dating anyone." Taylor's face flashed through her mind, a product of Cassie's insistence that he was romantically interested in her. She fought the urge to shake her head to rid herself of the thought.

"Then you're free for dinner?" he asked.

She sighed. "No. I'm actually a chef at one of the

restaurants in town, so I only get Mondays and Tuesdays off the dinner shift."

"Does this Monday work for you?" he asked. "I'd love to try out your favorite place for dinner, especially now that I know you're a chef. I'm sure you know all of the best places in town."

Her heart beat faster. She'd just been thinking about how static her life was currently, and then a stranger literally appeared in front of her and asked her out on a date. "Monday would be great." She smiled at him, hoping he didn't see her hand shaking as she lifted the coffee mug to her lips.

"Then Monday it is." He flashed her a grin. "I don't have a car to pick you up, but maybe we could meet at the entrance to the marina at six o'clock and walk somewhere for dinner?"

She nodded. "Sounds good." She finished the last sip of her coffee and stood. She needed to leave for work, but she found herself reluctant to leave this reprieve from her normal life. The odds were good that this traveler wouldn't even be in town by Monday, but she'd enjoyed his attention. "I'm sorry, but I really have to get to work. I'll see you on Monday, okay?"

"I'm looking forward to it." He stood and shook her hand. "It was nice to meet you, Meg."

"It was nice meeting you too." She turned to leave, but hesitated. What exactly was the correct protocol for leaving when you'd just made a dinner date with a stranger? Telling him it was nice to meet him felt a little cold when they'd made plans to get together at a later date. "See you later."

He smiled and gave her a half wave, then reached for his coffee.

She walked away with a bounce in her step. Maybe

this was it, the catalyst for change in her life. She looked back at Theo. His eyes were on the boats sailing past on the river channel – not on her. A touch of irrational sadness hit her. With their fairy-tale meeting, she'd found herself hoping he'd be so enchanted with her that he would want to keep her in sight until she was out of view.

On the sidewalk outside, Meg wove her way between throngs of tourists as she hurried toward Willa Bay Drive and the Lodge. Her phone rang in her purse, and she answered it as soon as she saw who was calling. "Libby? Aren't you supposed to be camping this weekend?"

"I am. My phone's actually getting reception at our campsite today." Libby went quiet on the other end of the line.

Meg waited a moment to see if she wasn't hearing her sister due to bad reception at the campground, then asked, "Libby, are you okay?"

Libby sighed, her breath coming through the phone in a reverberating puff of air. "Everything's fine. I was just a little lonely here and thought I might catch you before work to chat for a few minutes."

Meg glanced at her watch. Less than ten minutes to get to the Lodge before her shift started. She picked up the pace, her sneakers slapping rhythmically against the pavement. "Where is Gabe? And the kids? How are you lonely on a family camping trip?"

"He and the older kids all went fishing off the dock. Kaya is napping in the tent, so I stayed back with her. I needed to tidy up a little around here anyway." Libby's voice was fading in and out, and Meg pictured her buzzing around the campsite, picking up and rearranging things as she went.

"How is Gabe?" Meg lowered her voice, although she wasn't sure why, because there wasn't anyone else around.

She'd always thought of her sister as perfect, but recently a crack had appeared in her flawless veneer, and Libby had admitted to having fears that her husband was having an affair. Meg still didn't think Gabe was cheating, but from what Libby had told her, something wasn't quite right with him.

"He complained about coming here yesterday and even lashed out at me about the cost of the tent, but he seems to be coming around now." Something clattered in the background. "Fiddlesticks," Libby said.

"What was that?" Meg asked as she entered the long driveway leading to the Lodge.

"A pan I'd just washed fell on the ground." Libby clanked some pots together. "At home, I'd probably have washed it again, but out here, I just wiped off the pine needles and set it back on the table."

Meg couldn't quite stifle a chuckle. "You're such a rebel."

"Oh, be quiet." Libby laughed too. "I'm not always as uptight as you think I am."

"I know." Meg walked past one of the many flowerbeds on the Lodge's property, inhaling the scent of gardenias, one of her favorites. "But I still like to tease you about it."

She stopped in front of the employee entrance at the back the Lodge. "Libby, I'm at work now. Can we talk later?"

"Oh. I was hoping we could chat a little longer." Libby was quiet for a moment, then her voice rang out with false brightness. "But I know you need to get to work, and the kids should be back soon anyway. I should probably enjoy the quiet while I can."

Meg checked her watch. She needed to clock in ASAP. "Are you sure?"

"Of course. I'll talk to you later. Maybe tomorrow

when we get home." Libby hung up before Meg could say goodbye.

Meg stared at her phone, her heart sinking into her stomach. One of the things she'd appreciated about moving back to Willa Bay was the opportunity to be around more for friends and family. With all of her commitments, though, she was quickly losing that.

With a sigh, she pulled open the door to the Lodge and stepped inside, ready to begin her late lunch and dinner shift. In the kitchen, she found Taylor alternating between tending to a pot on the stove and chopping carrots.

He looked up when she entered. "Hey, Meg. Tonight's going to be busy. We're almost fully booked for dinner."

"Really?" She clocked in and slid her chef's coat over her tank top. "Is there an event tonight?"

"Nope, just the normal tourist traffic." He shot her an easy grin that made her heart skip a beat. Taylor may not have been as charmingly handsome as Theo, but he always made her feel at ease.

She stopped in her tracks, her head buzzing at that thought. Why was she even comparing the two of them? Taylor was a nice guy, but he was her boss. There was never going to be anything between the two of them, even if he *was* interested in her. Had her brief interaction with Theo turned her into an even bigger romantic than Cassie?

Taylor cocked his head to the side, holding his knife in the air. "Uh, are you okay?"

She wrenched her attention away from thoughts of him and forced a smile. Having Theo come into her life had seemed like divine intervention, but maybe she didn't have the mental energy for that kind of thing right now. "Sorry, I have a lot on my mind."

He nodded. "I totally get it." He looked around the kitchen, settling on the stack of vegetables next to him. "Can you help me chop these, please? The seafood delivery we received today is so fresh that I half expect it to jump back into the ocean, so we're making pasta primavera with shrimp. I have a feeling it's going to be our most popular dish tonight."

Meg nodded, then grabbed a knife and got into position at the counter about two feet away from Taylor. She tried to focus, but after her recent thoughts about his physical appearance, standing so close to him was messing with her concentration. Fortunately, he finished what he was doing and moved on to a task across the room. She glanced at him and breathed a sigh of relief. This date with Theo would be good for her. With any luck, he'd erase any romantic notions about Taylor from her mind.

8

Cassie

Cassie closed her eyes and turned her face up to the sun, letting the warmth soak into her skin. After church, she'd changed out of her good sundress and into old denim overalls that were more appropriate for helping Zoe paint the railing on the back porch of the Inn. The kids were with Kyle for the weekend, and she'd had a good time at church with Celia that morning. With the combination of a sky so blue that no threat of rain was in the picture and a slight breeze off the bay, conditions were perfect for painting the railings.

Even Zoe, who'd lately been wired even more tightly than normal, seemed in a good mood. She set two cans of white paint on the ground and stuck a paintbrush on top of each, then took a deep breath and smiled at Cassie. "Thanks for helping today." Zoe pulled her hair back into a high ponytail before prying the first paint can open with the tip of a butter knife. "I feel like we're getting further behind on our renovations every day."

Cassie looked up at the Inn. The roof still didn't look too great, but the sun reflected brightly off the newly hung double-pane windows. The old gazebo had been leveled to the foundation, and a pile of new lumber sat on the ground next to it. A set of sawhorses had been placed nearby. In general, conditions at the Inn had vastly improved over the last few months.

"I think it looks good," Cassie said. "Is the roof going to be fixed soon? Weren't you having problems with it?"

Zoe's brow creased as she frowned. "The company Shawn hired had a delay on another job and won't be able to get to us now until August. Apparently, that's a frequent occurrence for that company, so I don't know why he hired them." She jammed the knife into the indentation in the top of the other can and roughly pried it loose, then threw the knife on the ground next to the paintbrush. "It drives me crazy when vendors don't honor their contracts, and it puts my plans all out of whack."

"Oh." Cassie eyed the moss-covered shingles on the porch roof. It seemed she'd hit a nerve. "Well, I'm sure it'll be fine to wait until August. We haven't had much rain this summer anyway."

"Yeah, luckily." Zoe glared at the roof, then dipped her brush into the paint. She swiped the bristles along the side of the railing, immediately coloring the wood with a bright white hue that contrasted sharply with the unpainted post next to it. "There's so much damage to the walls in the rooms upstairs that I haven't wanted Shawn to work on them much until we get the roof fixed. And we kind of need guest rooms before the Inn can open to the public."

Cassie covered her brush with paint and smoothed it over a post about four feet away from where Zoe was working. "I'm sure it will all get done. I know you, Zoe, and you'll make it happen."

Zoe gave her a small smile. "Thanks, Cass. I appreciate the support. Speaking of projects, are you getting excited about the bakery? When do you take possession of it?"

"At the end of the month." Cassie's heart fluttered. It was only a little over a week away until Edgar handed over the keys to the bakery. She'd gone back during the week when it wasn't so busy and took a few pictures of the layout. Now she was trying to figure out what changes she wanted to make. Unless she decided to do a major remodel, the counter would have to stay in its current location, but she planned to move some of the tables and other fixtures to improve the flow of traffic.

"Starting your own business is scary isn't it?" Zoe's eyes drilled into Cassie's face, warming her cheeks.

"It is." Cassie let her hands find a rhythm with long, even strokes of the brush against the wood, reloading paint on the bristles as needed. Remembering she was standing outside Celia's house, she lowered her voice. "Sometimes I can't believe I let Celia talk me into it."

Zoe laughed. "She's quite convincing when there's something on her agenda. I often find myself wondering if Meg, Shawn, and I actually came up with the idea to buy the Inn from her ourselves, or if she somehow planted the thought subconsciously."

"Probably a little of both." Cassie chuckled along with Zoe. Celia could be stubborn when she wanted to be, but Cassie knew she had her best interests at heart. If anything, Cassie was more worried about letting Celia down if the business failed. "But I gave my notice on Friday, so I'm stuck with my decision now." Her stomach lurched. Without her paycheck from the Lodge to depend on, she was solely dependent on her ability to turn a profit with the bakery.

"Good for you." Zoe stepped back to admire her work, then dabbed at a small spot she'd missed on one of the slats. "When I gave notice to George that I was quitting my job there, it was thrilling to think about my future here at the Inn, but it also made me feel like I was going to vomit."

Cassie smiled. "That's exactly how I felt. I've always dreamed of opening my own bakery, but I didn't expect it to happen so fast. If I'd been left to my own devices, I probably would have been sixty before I made the move."

"Yep," Zoe said. "Sometimes you just have to jump when the opportunity arises. I think that's why Celia had always been successful with the Inn, at least until her husband died. She has an uncanny knack for knowing when to adapt to new circumstances. Way back when she worked here as a maid, she knew things were changing, and the town would need to pivot to stay on the map." She swept her hand to encompass the grounds and toward the town of Willa Bay. "Without her suggesting to the Chamber of Commerce that the town focus on the wedding industry, everything you see in front of you would be waterfront condos, and none of the hotels or event venues in the area would exist."

Behind them, a saw roared to life. Cassie turned to watch as Shawn cut into a two-by-four, the blade zipping through the thick lumber like it was nothing. He set the neatly split wood near the foundation of the gazebo before consulting a piece of paper he'd removed from his pocket.

"You're lucky Shawn's good at construction," Cassie said. "I wouldn't even know where to start."

Zoe beamed, and her eyes softened as she gazed at her

boyfriend. "I know. He's a lifesaver around here." She sighed. "I shouldn't be so hard on him about the roofing company. He couldn't have known they'd be that flakey, and he's been working so hard. Last night, he fell asleep on the couch while we were watching TV."

"You've all been working hard," Cassie observed. "Meg looks like a zombie when she arrives for her shift at the Lodge."

Zoe sighed. "I need to remember that she's working another job too. I've found myself getting frustrated because it feels like I'm making all the decisions around here and have that huge weight hanging around my shoulders. Potential clients have inquired about holding their weddings here, but I haven't had time to show them around." She uttered a harsh laugh. "And I'm supposed to be the resident wedding planner." She looked over at the gazebo again. "I can't wait until I can get back to that. It makes me a little sad that I'm not around to see all the summer weddings at the Lodge that I coordinated. I put so much effort into each one of them, and I never dreamed I wouldn't be there to see them to fruition."

"Life doesn't always work out the way you plan." Cassie set her brush down and wrapped her arm around her friend's shoulders to give her a side hug. "But sometimes it's even better. Think of everything you have going for you now." She pointed at Shawn. "You have this amazing man in your life, you're a part-owner of the Inn, and you're well on your way to making this the best wedding venue in the entire town."

"I know." Zoe leaned in toward Cassie. "I need to remember that when everything feels out of my control." She cleared her throat. "I'm getting hungry. Let's finish painting this section and have some lunch, okay? I think

Celia has something going in the Crockpot in the living room."

Cassie raised her eyebrows. "The living room?"

"The kitchen remodel is scheduled to last for another month." Zoe shrugged. "Celia's pretty much turned the living room into a makeshift kitchen and seems happy as a clam. I told you she adapted easily to new situations."

Cassie laughed. "Well, I'm looking forward to whatever she's cooking. Anything I don't have to make is good with me."

They both got back to painting and quickly finished the whole railing on that side of the building.

Zoe stepped back. "Looks good." She reached for Cassie's paint brush. "If you can take care of closing up the cans, I'll take these inside to rinse off."

Cassie handed over her brush, then snapped the lids back on the cans as Zoe disappeared into the house. When she was done, she stood and took another look at the gazebo. Shawn had a ruler out, marking the wood with a pencil.

Kyle had never taken an interest in working with his hands, and getting him to do little fixes around the house, like oiling door hinges, had been painful. They'd once lived with a broken toilet seat for over a month before he replaced it. Now that he was no longer living with them, though, she realized how much he'd actually done while he was there. Her lips curved into a wistful half-smile as she remembered when he'd finally gone to replace the toilet seat. He'd tugged on it, and the old, brittle plastic screws had suddenly snapped, sending him flying backward. He'd slid down the wall, stunned, still holding the wooden ring. After the shock had worn off, they'd laughed about it for hours.

She turned her gaze back to the Inn. Maybe she'd

remarry in the future, but for now, home improvement projects were up to her. If anything came up that she couldn't handle, she had the phone number for a local handyman.

"Ready for lunch?" Zoe asked as she opened the door. "Celia made a bacon mac 'n' cheese that smells amazing."

The aroma of melting cheese wafted through the open door, and Cassie's stomach grumbled. They'd skipped the coffee hour after church so Cassie would have more time to help Zoe with painting. "I could eat a horse at this point."

Zoe wrinkled her nose. "Gross. I think I'll stick with the mac 'n' cheese." She came down the steps. "I'm going to let Shawn know lunch is ready, then we'll be right in."

Cassie nodded. "I'll try to save you some food, but I'm not making any promises if you take too long."

"Haha." Zoe smiled. "I'll see you inside." She strode off toward Shawn.

Cassie moved the paint cans against the Inn's foundation, watching Zoe and Shawn in her peripheral vision. Zoe approached Shawn, and he shot her a welcoming smile as he put down the piece of wood he'd been working with. The tension eased visibly from Zoe's shoulders as she stood on her tiptoes to kiss him on the lips.

Cassie averted her gaze, but the depth of affection between them filled her heart. Zoe had a good match in Shawn, even if she was upset with him about the roofers.

Once upon a time, things had been like that between Cassie and Kyle. An unexpected pang of sadness shot through her chest at the thought of what they'd lost, hitting her harder than usual because of how happy Zoe and Shawn looked together. She'd been thinking about Kyle more and more lately, softening to him as he fought to repair his relationship with the kids and salvage whatever remaining amity he had with her.

Not for the first time, she wondered if there was even a small chance that the two of them could work through their differences and regain the love they'd once shared. Having her family together was something she'd dreamed about, but deemed impossible. Then again, she'd thought the same thing about her chance of owning a bakery.

She took a deep breath and climbed up the stairs before she could delve more deeply into the feelings that were swirling around her like a cloud of fog. She pushed open the door and walked inside.

"Celia?" Cassie called out into the empty hallway.

"I'm in here," Celia answered from Cassie's left. "Follow your nose."

Cassie grinned and entered the living room. The seating area with the sofa, recliner, and TV had been condensed into a smaller space near the entry. Cooking paraphernalia covered a long table against the back wall and steam rose from a Crockpot at the far end. The small dining table from the kitchen had been moved onto a rug a few feet away, and now bore four place settings. Celia sat in one of the chairs, drinking from a mug of coffee.

Cassie crossed the room and sat down next to her. "It smells wonderful. Thanks for making lunch for all of us."

Celia's face lit up. "This is nothing compared to all the hard work everyone is putting in here. I'm so grateful to see all of the improvements. Feeding you all is the least I could do."

Shawn and Zoe soon arrived, and they all quickly polished off the macaroni and cheese. After they finished helping Celia clear away lunch, Zoe and Cassie returned to painting.

As they chatted, Cassie worked up the nerve to talk

about her recent conflicting emotions over her ex-husband. "I think I might still have feelings for Kyle," Cassie finally blurted out before she could stop herself.

Zoe stopped painting and looked at Cassie with surprise. "You mean like romantic feelings?"

Cassie nodded, not meeting Zoe's gaze.

"Wow." Zoe was silent for a minute. "You were pretty miserable with him, remember?"

"I know." Cassie took a deep breath. "But I think he's changed. He's really trying to be present now for the kids – and for me."

"I don't know if it's a good idea," Zoe said. "I mean, it's obviously your choice if you want to say something to him, but please think about it carefully."

"I will." It wasn't like Cassie wanted to have feelings for her ex, but she couldn't seem to get rid of them. She'd been confused enough before talking to Zoe. Now, after hearing her friend's opinion about Kyle, she almost wished she hadn't said anything to her about him.

They both went back to painting and chatting, studiously avoiding the subject of Kyle. By late afternoon, they'd completed all the railings that wrapped around the porch.

"Thanks, Cassie," Zoe said. "We really appreciate all of your help."

"No problem. I'm happy to help out." Cassie breathed in the fresh sea air, catching a whiff of paint in the process. "It was actually kind of fun."

"Well, if there's anything I can do to help with the bakery, let me know." Zoe looked at her notebook, which lay on an end table on the porch. "Though I don't know how much help I'll be for the next few months before the Inn is up and running."

Cassie smiled at her. "I will." She checked her watch. It

was almost four o'clock, so she still had an hour until Kyle would bring the kids home. She nodded to the paintbrushes. "Do you need any help with cleanup?"

Zoe shook her head. "Nope, I'm good. Thanks again for everything." Her expression turned serious. "And Cass?"

"Yeah?" Cassie cocked her head to the side.

"Sorry if I overstepped when you asked about Kyle. I didn't mean to sound so harsh about him, but I just worry about you. I don't want you to get hurt again."

Cassie's cheeks warmed, and she bit her lip, looking down at the green grass curling around the toes of her sneakers. "I know. I don't want to get hurt again either." She looked up to meet Zoe's gaze. "But if he's really changed and there's a chance for my family to be together again, I don't want to throw it away."

Zoe nodded. "I get it. Just be careful, okay?" She came over and gave Cassie an awkward hug, holding her paint streaked hands out to the side so she wouldn't stain Cassie's clothes.

Cassie gave her a small smile, then stepped back. "I'll be careful." She held up her own messy fingers and laughed. "But for now, I think I should be more worried about getting this paint smeared all over everything. I'm going to go get cleaned up in the house and say goodbye to Celia."

"Sounds good." Zoe gathered up the supplies, and they walked into the house through the back door, which opened into a laundry room with a wide utility sink. On a counter by the sink, the Crockpot insert had been washed and turned upside down on a hand towel. Nearby, a makeshift shelf on the wall held an assortment of plates and glass cups.

Zoe rinsed off the paintbrushes, then looked around

for a good place to set them to dry. She eyed the dishes. "I'm going to be so happy once the kitchen remodel is done."

"I bet Celia will be too," Cassie said. "This has to be a big change for her."

"I know. At least I can still cook in my cottage," Zoe said. "I offered to make some meals for her, but she wouldn't hear of it." She smiled. "That's Celia for you. Stubborn as ever."

"Speaking of Celia, I'd better get going." Cassie washed up, then said goodbye to Zoe. She walked down the hallway to the living room, where Celia was watching TV with Pebbles.

Celia's head turned toward the hall. "How'd the painting go, dear?"

Cassie smiled. "It went well. We got all of the railings done." She walked over and rubbed Pebbles between the ears. He pressed his head into her hand, urging her to continue petting him. She gave him a few pats on the back, then looked up at Celia. "Kyle's dropping off the kids soon, so I need to get home. I'll see you next Sunday for church, okay?"

Celia nodded intently. "I'll be ready. I'm looking forward to seeing the kids again."

"Me too." Cassie laughed. "I can't believe how much I miss those little monsters when they're at their dad's house for the weekend."

A wistful expression came over Celia's face. "I know the feeling."

Cassie's heart dropped. Celia did know what it felt like to miss a child. She'd given her daughter up for adoption as a baby and had only recently become acquainted with her grandchild. "I'm sorry, I wasn't thinking."

Celia's eyes drilled into Cassie's face. "There's nothing

to be sorry about. I imagine it would be very difficult to have your house so full of the children's energy one day and then so very quiet the next. Young people are such a joy to be around."

Cassie suppressed a smirk. She wasn't sure she'd call them a "joy," but she did miss her children, even the constant bickering between them.

Celia waved her hand in the air. "Thank you for the ride today. It's so nice to see all my church friends every week."

"I'm happy to do it." Cassie flashed Celia a smile, then leaned in to give Pebbles a final pet. "I'll see you next week." She walked out to her car, filled with a renewed sense of excitement at the thought of seeing her kids. Although she enjoyed having time to herself when they were with Kyle, the house seemed so quiet and lonely without them. Maybe it was time to get a dog to keep her company.

9

Kyle

"Jace is hitting me," Amanda yelled from the backseat.

"She started it!" Jace shouted back.

Kyle looked into the rearview mirror and shook his head. They glared at each other with a fierce stubbornness that reminded him of Cassie. "Knock it off, both of you!" He continued driving down Main Street, then turned off toward Cassie's house. "We're almost home."

"Good!" Amanda said. "I can't wait to get away from him."

"Me too," Jace said. Kyle caught a glimpse of him sticking out his tongue.

"Gross!" Amanda squeezed herself into the corner of the car as far away from her brother as possible.

Kyle gritted his teeth. The weekend had started out fine, but by Sunday afternoon the kids had spent far too much time together. Since he only had them every other weekend, he tried to maximize his time with them by filling it with as many fun activities as possible – like going to museums, out to eat, or to the movies. However, to lessen the strain between his two very different children, it might be better in the future for all of them to hang out at his apartment for some of that time so they could do things apart for a while.

He pulled up in front of Cassie's house. She'd planted some new flowers over the weekend, and they added a nice pop of color against the siding. He'd never been much for gardening, but she'd always had an affinity for it.

"We're here," he said.

The kids spilled out of their seats, pushing past each other to get to the front door.

He sighed and got out, popping open the trunk grumbling in a low voice, "That's fine, don't bother to help with all of your stuff." He plucked the suitcases out and set them on the sidewalk. Both kids stood on the front porch with Cassie, talking rapidly as they each told her what the other sibling had done to wrong them.

Cassie smiled patiently, her wavy blonde hair floating softly around her shoulders. Her complexion seemed rosier than usual, as though she'd recently spent time in the sun, and a speck of white paint dotted her cheek. Her simple cotton sundress brought back memories of the summers they'd shared as teenagers, and his chest tightened. She held up her hand. "Okay, okay. You've both done things to each other."

Amanda opened her mouth as if to protest, but Cassie wrapped her arms around both of the kids before Amanda could utter a word. "I missed you guys," Cassie said.

"We missed you too," Amanda admitted.

Cassie released them and smiled at Kyle. "So, what exciting things did the three of you do this weekend?"

Jace's face lit up. "We saw the new Star Wars movie!"

Kyle nodded. "And ate about four gallons of popcorn and loads of candy while we were at the theater."

Cassie's eyebrows lifted. "Sounds fun."

"It was," Amanda said. "And we went swimming in the pool at Dad's apartment complex."

Jace nodded, then darted inside the house.

"Bye, buddy," Kyle called after him.

"Bye, Dad." Jace's voice floated out the door.

"Well, I'm glad you got some exercise." Cassie grinned at Kyle. "And I'm happy you three had fun. I hung out at the Inn with Zoe today, painting. It was a beautiful day to be outside, but now all I want is a hot bath."

That explained the splotch of paint on her cheek. "How are things going out there?" Kyle checked the time on his phone while he waited for her to answer. He'd promised Dana he'd meet her at the bowling alley at five fifteen for a burger before they rented a lane. It was their first date, but, surprisingly, he wasn't terribly nervous about it.

"Things are coming along." She nodded to his phone. "Got somewhere to be?"

His eyes met hers. "Yeah, in a little bit. I'm meeting a friend for dinner."

"A friend?" Cassie stared at him, her blue eyes open wide. He shifted uncomfortably in his Oxford loafers.

Amanda rolled her eyes. "Dad has a hot date with some woman from work."

He glanced at Cassie, who'd winced perceptibly at Amanda's statement. Heat rose up from his collar. "It's not a hot date. I mean, I guess it's a date, but ..."

Amanda groaned. "I don't need to hear about my dad dating."

He pressed his lips together. "Well, that's great,

because *I* don't need to share all the details of my personal life with you."

He glanced at Cassie. She didn't look at him directly but flashed him a small smile and said, "Have fun tonight." She ushered Amanda into the house and grabbed the suitcases. "Let's let Daddy get going." With a quick wave, she went inside and closed the door.

He shoved his hands into his jeans pockets and pivoted on the sidewalk, returning to his car. The whole way to the bowling alley, he kept replaying their interaction. Was Cassie upset that he was dating again? They'd been divorced for two years – it was time for both of them to see other people. His stomach twisted. Cassie had made it clear that she didn't have any interest in getting back together. He needed to move forward with his life, and going out with Dana was a good way to start that process.

When he got to the bowling alley, he texted Dana. *Are you here?*

She replied right away. *Yes! I nabbed us a table in the bar.*

He stuffed his phone into his pocket and walked toward the door, his steps slowing the closer he got to the entrance. The realization finally hit him that this *was* a date. He'd socialized with Dana at work events many times over the years, but tonight it would be just the two of them.

A group of kids overtook him, and he stepped out of their way, taking a moment to compose his thoughts. This was what he wanted, wasn't it? Dana was an intelligent and attractive woman, and any man would be happy to go out on a date with her.

He took a deep breath, then approached the door with resolve and pulled it open with a firm grasp on the handle. He strode toward the bar at the back of the bowling alley, his confidence growing. As he neared the open seating area, Dana stood up from a small table near the far wall and waved, smiling widely at him before sitting back down.

He waved back and made his way across the crowded restaurant to her. "They're busy tonight."

She scanned the room. "Yeah, I think there's a bowling league here, but I already reserved a lane for us. We should have about an hour to eat."

He nodded. "Good thinking." The strategic and organizational skills that made her an excellent tax accountant clearly also made her a great planner. He sat down across from her and selected a menu from a metal stand on top of the napkin dispenser. "Have you been here before? I wonder if their burgers are any good."

He'd been to the bowling alley with his kids, but he'd never eaten in the bar with them. They usually just grabbed slices of pizza and soda pop from the quick service counter situated closer to the lanes.

She nodded. "I've been here a few times. My brother used to play in one of the leagues before he moved out of town." She scanned the menu. "The burgers I've had have been pretty good. I think I'm going to try the Bacon and Blue Burger tonight."

He swallowed against a suddenly dry throat. That was Cassie's favorite. Finding a restaurant that served a good hamburger with bacon and blue cheese always made her face light up.

"Are you okay?" Dana peered at him.

He smiled. "I'm fine. I was just thinking that I'll have to tell Cassie they have those on the menu. She loves them."

Dana set her menu down and tilted her head to the side. "Your ex-wife?"

He froze. Probably not a good idea to be talking about

his ex when he was out with someone else. "Yeah, I saw her earlier when I dropped off the kids, so she popped into my mind when you mentioned that burger."

She narrowed her eyes slightly and picked up the menu. "Uh-huh. Well, that'll be nice of you to tell her."

He let his breath out slowly and returned his attention to his own menu. The entrée descriptions were swimming in front of him, but he made himself focus long enough to choose something. He clapped his menu shut. "I think I'm going to get the one with the onion ring and barbecue sauce."

"Oh, that one's good." Dana smiled at him, seeming to have forgiven him for his earlier faux pas of mentioning his ex on a first date. Besides, it wasn't like Dana didn't know about Cassie's existence. They'd been working together for a decade, and he'd been married for most of that.

The waitress came to take their orders, promising their food would be ready in about thirty minutes.

"So," Dana said, folding her arms in front of her on the table. "How has your weekend been?"

"So far, so good." He grinned at her. "I took the kids to the new Star Wars movie, and we had a blast."

"Oh, how fun!" She took a sip of her Pepsi. "I was planning on seeing that soon." Her eyes danced. "Any chance you want to see it again?"

He reached for his beer, hoping to stall a little. This was their first date, and she was already talking about going out in the future. It wasn't that he didn't like her, but he was still getting used to the idea of being out on a date in the first place.

She reached out and patted the table near him. "Hey, sorry. I didn't mean to scare you. I know you haven't dated much since you and Cassie split."

He nodded. "Thanks. Sorry if I'm a bit rusty at this."

She shook her head. "Not at all. We've been friends for a long time. I get it."

His chest warmed, and he relaxed into his chair. They *had* been friends for a long time. Being on a date with Dana didn't have to be weird. She was still the same person he'd known for practically forever. "So, do you think they'll finally announce the promotions this week?"

She shrugged and gulped her soda. "You'd think so. I know Cliff was out of town last week, but c'mon, we need to know soon!" She leaned forward. "Don't tell anyone, but on Friday, I had a recruiter approach me about a job with a firm in Seattle."

He sat back. "Are you thinking about taking it?"

She shrugged again. "I'm not sure. If I don't get promoted, then yeah, I'm definitely going to consider it." She sighed. "I don't know. I've never really pictured myself working in Willa Bay long-term. If I'm going to jump to a new firm, this would be a good time."

He gestured to the length of the bowling alley. "What, and leave all this?"

Dana laughed. "I know, right?" She looked at him intently. "You grew up here, didn't you? Don't you ever dream of going somewhere else? Moving to a bigger town? I know Cassie never wanted to move, but now that you're not together, you can leave Willa Bay."

Kyle surveyed the bowling alley. In a single sweeping glance, he recognized at least twenty people, including a few guys he'd grown up with. Could he leave Willa Bay? With the exception of his time in college, it was all he'd ever known.

He reached for his napkin, damp with condensation from his drink, and twisted it between his fingers. "I don't know. I haven't thought about it much. My kids are here, so I wouldn't want to go too far."

"Well, the economy is great right now, and with your experience you could get a job at any number of firms. You could go anywhere in the Puget Sound area and still be able to see your kids when it was your weekend with them." She smiled at him, noticing his hesitation. "Sorry, I didn't mean to drag the mood down. I'm just excited about the possibility of moving." She added hastily, "I haven't made any decisions yet, though."

"I'm happy for you. It's always nice to be in demand." He met her gaze. "I hadn't considered it before, but you've given me something to think about."

The waitress came by and set plates full of burgers and fries in front of them.

Dana bit into her burger, and her eyes rolled up with pleasure. "Okay, this is amazing." She took another huge bite, while Kyle sampled his. "How's yours?"

"It's good." In actuality, he was too preoccupied, and could have been eating a leather shoe for all he tasted. He alternated between the sandwich and the fries, his thoughts stuck on what Dana had suggested.

Could he move away from Willa Bay? Besides his kids, he didn't have much keeping him there. He liked his job okay, but he could find one somewhere else. His small apartment sufficed, but it wasn't home. An image of the house he'd shared with Cassie flashed into his mind. Would anywhere else ever be home?

"It looks like you enjoyed it," Dana said, bringing him back to the present.

Kyle looked down at his plate, surprised to see that only one fry remained. He dipped it into the smidge of ketchup that remained and popped it into his mouth. "I did." He grabbed a new napkin from the holder in front of him and wiped off his hands, while looking over at her empty plate. "You seemed to like yours too."

She laughed. "I did. I think we were both so hungry that we ploughed through them and forgot anyone else was here."

Guilt washed over him. He'd been so caught up in his own thoughts that he'd neglected her. "Sorry," he said with a sheepish grin.

"No worries." She looked at the huge clock on the wall. "Our lane opens up in about twenty minutes. I hope the waitress gets over here soon with our bill."

He raised his hand to flag down the waitress. She came over to them and looked at their plates. "I'm guessing everything tasted good? Is there anything else I can get you?"

"The food was great." Kyle smiled at her. "I think we're pretty full, though. Can we please get our bill?"

"Of course." She reached into her pocket and pulled out a handful of paper slips, then handed one to him. "You can pay up at the register."

"Thank you," he said. He and Dana both stood and walked over to the cashier, where Kyle paid for their meal, leaving a generous tip. He'd worked at one of the cafés in town when he was in high school and knew how hard the waitstaff worked.

"Thanks for dinner," Dana said. "The shoe rentals and lane are on me."

He grinned. "Sounds like a fair trade."

They rented their shoes, selected bowling balls, then made their way over to their assigned lane.

Kyle hefted his bowling ball in the air to test the weight. "I have to warn you, I'm not a great bowler."

She laughed. "Me neither, but I always have fun."

He released his ball down the lane, and they watched

as it rolled straight toward the pins. At the last moment, it veered left and only took down half of them.

"Not bad," she said.

They continued playing through to the last frame, Dana narrowly beating Kyle by a few points. Then they returned their shoes and walked out of the bowling alley into the parking lot.

"Good game," Kyle said.

"I kind of impressed myself. I've never done that well. You must be a good-luck charm." She grinned up at him.

"Yeah, I get that a lot." He laughed, then nodded in the direction of his car. "Did you drive here?"

She shook her head. "No, I walked. My apartment isn't too far away." She motioned to the street behind them. "Only a few blocks down Eighth Street."

"I can give you a ride," he suggested. "Or I could walk you home."

She gave him a long, assessing look. "A walk would be nice. Thanks."

They walked side by side until they reached her apartment on the first floor of a small building. She inserted her key in the lock and turned it, then looked up at him. "I had a nice time tonight."

He automatically said, "Me too," only then realizing that he really had enjoyed being on a date with Dana. They'd always been good friends, so maybe there was a chance for more between them.

She hesitated, then stretched up to kiss him quickly on the mouth. "Thanks for tonight." She darted into her apartment before he could answer.

"Goodnight," he called to her as the door was closing.

She stuck her head out, her eyes dancing. "See you tomorrow."

"See you tomorrow," Kyle said.

The door shut, and he walked away slowly. She'd kissed him. It was the first time he'd been kissed by a woman who wasn't Cassie or someone related to him. It had been so quick that he hadn't known what to think at the time, but it hadn't been what he would have expected. Her lips had been soft and her touch light, but he hadn't experienced that same zing of attraction when their lips touched that he'd always had when kissing Cassie.

You're older now, he reminded himself. He and Cassie had been high school sweethearts. He couldn't expect to find the same sort of all-consuming passion that he'd known as a teenager.

So what if that feeling had persisted through their first few years of marriage? He and Cassie had split up because they'd grown apart instead of growing together. They weren't the same people they'd been as teenagers, and they weren't right for each other now.

His heart clenched, and he forced himself to think about the future. It was time for him to stop focusing on what might have been and move on with his life. This first kiss may have been lackluster, but Dana was a beautiful, attractive woman, and any future kisses were sure to be better.

10

Zoe

Zoe watched from the beach as Shawn, assisted by a man he'd hired to help, hoisted a pre-constructed section of rafters to the top of the gazebo's frame. For as long as she'd lived on the property, she'd loved seeing the antique wedding gazebo perched high above the beach, overlooking the deep blue waters of Willa Bay. She imagined all of the happy occasions it had already witnessed, and dreamed about seeing it as the centerpiece for future weddings at the resort.

Tearing down the old building had pained her, but the original wood frame had rotted out and couldn't be saved. In its place, a new pavilion sprouted from the earth like the flowers growing and blossoming along the base of the Inn's porch. In time, climbing roses would be planted around the gazebo's foundation, intertwining through the latticework to lend privacy to the structure's interior.

Pebbles tugged at the leash, and Zoe looked down at

him. He gave her a doggy grin, then trotted off down the beach, pulling the line taut.

"Hey, wait for me." She jogged after him along the hard-packed sand near the surf. With every step of her sneaker-clad feet hitting the ground, her anxiety eased. There were so many projects on her renovation schedule that were not going according to plan. Seeing the progress on the gazebo made all of that seem less worrisome, at least temporarily.

Zoe and Pebbles continued their walk for another twenty minutes before climbing the stairs up from the beach. On the way back to the Inn, she took a closer look at the gazebo. The hired helper was standing on a ladder, fastening the final rafter onto the frame, but Shawn wasn't there.

"Hello," Zoe called out.

The man looked down at her and smiled. "Good morning." Small hand tools hung from a belt around his waist, and he looked as comfortable balancing on the rung of the ladder as Zoe did on terra firma.

"It's really coming along." Zoe scanned the structure, her chest filling with pride. She could hardly wait until they were able to host events at the Inn. "It'll be gorgeous when it's finished."

"It will be." He turned slightly and fondly patted the nearest support. "With proper maintenance, this beauty should last you for the next fifty years." He looked down at her again, grinning at Pebbles, who was straining at the leash and yipping at a robin hopping on the grass about ten feet away. "I think he's ready to go. Did you need something?"

She laughed, reining in Pebbles so he wouldn't scare the bird. "I was wondering if you knew where Shawn went?"

He shrugged. "He got a phone call from someone and said he needed to meet with them for an hour or so." He pointed behind them. "The last time I saw him, he was walking toward the Inn."

She flashed him a smile. "Thanks."

"No problem." He pulled a hammer out of his pocket and tapped on a nail that wasn't quite flush.

Zoe let Pebbles lead her away and indulged him for a few minutes in his quest to find the robin, who'd since flown to safety in a nearby tree. On the other side of the Inn, someone had parked an unfamiliar car in the circular gravel driveway. Was this Shawn's mystery guest? Was it a potential contractor? Her spirits rose. Maybe it was a roofing company.

"Pebbles! Time to go home." She tugged at the leash, and he reluctantly followed her up to the front door and into the house.

Once inside, she unclipped his harness, and he ran off down the hall, probably searching for Celia. The voices of Shawn and an unfamiliar woman floated toward her from out of the living room. Zoe knocked on the closed door before peeking her head in. The two of them were seated at the dining table. The woman, who appeared to be in her late twenties, was dressed professionally in a fitted cap-sleeve blouse over a floral calf-length skirt. And, of all things, they were chatting about weddings at the Inn.

Zoe entered the room, closing the door behind her and walking over to them. "Hello." Ordinarily, she wouldn't interrupt Shawn when he was meeting with a contractor, but all the contractors she'd met previously lived in a uniform of jeans and a T-shirt, and she'd never heard them mention weddings.

Shawn gestured for her to join them. "Zoe, I want you to meet Tia. She's a wedding planner too."

Zoe held out her hand and smiled politely at the woman, but she still wasn't sure what was going on. "Nice to meet you, Tia."

Tia shook Zoe's hand with a firm grasp. "Nice to meet you too."

"Do you have time to join us?" Shawn asked Zoe.

She looked between the two of them. "Uh, sure."

Shawn pulled out the chair next to him, and she sat down, folding her hands in her lap.

"I know how much stress you've been under with the renovations, and it's only going to get worse as you start meeting with potential clients prior to our grand opening." His eyes were full of concern, and Zoe's heart melted. She was constantly amazed with how attuned he was to her needs.

She nodded. "True. But I can handle it."

Shawn gave her a half-smile. "I know you can, but I don't think you should have to do it on your own. Meg and I are both so busy, and, frankly, we're a little out of our element when it comes to planning events." He cast a glance at Tia. "I was thinking it might be good to bring someone else on to help you with potential clients."

Ice ran through her veins. Prior to quitting her job at the Willa Bay Lodge, she'd been in line for the event manager position – that is, until the owner's son-in-law had been offered it instead. The Inn at Willa Bay was her baby – her chance to create the premier wedding venue in the area. She fought to control her reaction and speak diplomatically. "I don't think I need any help with events."

Shawn and Tia exchanged glances.

"Do you mind if I speak with Zoe alone?" Shawn asked Tia.

Tia's gaze flitted over to Zoe, then back to Shawn. "No, of course not." She eyed the window overlooking the front porch. "Actually, if you don't mind, I'd love to check out the grounds. When I arrived, I saw some beautiful flowers I'd like to get a closer look at."

Shawn nodded. "I'll meet you out there in a bit."

Tia stood and exited the room. From the hallway outside the living room came a faint click as the front door latched shut behind her.

Zoe turned to Shawn. "You went behind my back to hire someone to take my place?" Her gut ached like she'd been kicked, and unseen pressure squeezed at her ribcage. What had Shawn been thinking? He had to have known she wouldn't want this.

"I wasn't trying to go behind your back. Cassie mentioned that Tia was new in town and interested in taking on more clients. I know you've been stressed lately, and I thought this might take some of the burden off of you." He searched her face.

She glared back at him. "So, you *don't* think I can handle it."

He sighed. "No, it's not that – really." He reached his hand out to her, but she didn't move any closer. "Look, we don't have to hire Tia, but can you please give the idea a chance? She seems like a nice woman and could be a huge help to you – and all of us."

Zoe pushed her chair back from the table and got to her feet. "I can already tell you, my answer is no."

"Zoe ..." Shawn implored. "Please consider it."

She shook her head. "I need to get out of here for a few minutes." She'd just been outside, but the walls of the house were closing in on her, and she felt an overwhelming urge to leave. "I'll talk to you later, okay? Please tell Tia it was nice to meet her."

In hopes of not running into Tia – or anyone else, for that matter – she exited the house via the back door. Once outside, she gulped in the fresh air and walked rapidly across the grassy lawn to the safety of the woods surrounding the cottages along the cliff. Instead of entering her own home, she continued on past it.

Most of the other cottages were run-down and hadn't been occupied in years, but Shawn had recently moved out of the main guest house and into a cottage close to hers, which he'd fixed up to a livable condition. After the current renovations were complete, they planned to remodel the barn into a restaurant and then would focus their third phase of construction on the row of cottages on the cliff.

Zoe picked her way around the tree branches and brambles that had taken over the road. Once upon a time, it had been a one-lane gravel path, just wide enough to allow the resort's guests to access their accommodations by vehicle. She kept going until she'd passed the last building, almost on the edge of the resort's property, then ducked through a gap in the overgrown brush. When she emerged, she was standing in the middle of a small, natural clearing.

She'd discovered this spot last summer, and it had become one of her favorite places. She climbed onto the trunk of a massive tree that must have fallen during a storm years ago. Up here, she had a bird's-eye view of the entire stretch of beach below the resort, and could even catch a peek of the marina miles down the road.

She leaned against a sturdy tree branch and hugged her legs to her chest. Bringing the Inn back to life was a dream she'd never thought possible. But here she was, a part-owner of the resort, and with any luck, they'd be hosting their first guests in a few months. The Inn would offer the most beautiful and special wedding venue in all of Willa Bay, and she was a part of it. So why did everything seem so hard?

Had she made a mistake in quitting her job at the Lodge? After the owner's son-in-law had taken over managing events there, she'd been miserable at work. But it had been a steady paycheck, and she hadn't been responsible for renovating an entire resort and promoting it to potential guests.

She'd never been so naive to think owning a resort with her friend and new boyfriend wouldn't come with its own hardships, but she hadn't expected it to be this difficult. Meg wasn't around as much as Zoe would like, but that wasn't Meg's fault either. They'd jointly made the decision for Meg to keep her job for the time being.

Zoe sighed. Most of all, she worried about how the stress of renovations was affecting her new relationship with Shawn. She didn't want this to come between them, but with the roofing debacle and Shawn bringing Tia to the Inn, it had.

She was under a lot of pressure, though, and she knew Shawn had only been trying to protect her. Had she overreacted? She stretched out her legs and wiggled them awake before jumping down to the ground. Whatever the case, avoiding Shawn wasn't going to make anything better.

11

Cassie

Cassie stared at her computer screen. Maybe if she focused on them for long enough, the numbers on her spreadsheet would change. No matter how she arranged the figures, money would be tight after she received her last steady paycheck from the Willa Bay Lodge. She glanced at the Mickey Mouse calendar on the wall above the desk in her kitchen. Only one more week. One more week, and she'd officially be self-employed.

She rubbed her eyes and leaned back in her chair. It had been a long day already, and the kids would be home from school any minute. From the desk, her cell phone buzzed, and an unfamiliar number filled the lit screen.

"Hello?" she answered.

"Hi, Cassie. This is Andy with Avery Construction."

"Oh, hi." She and Andy had both grown up in Willa Bay and had been friends since elementary school. When Cassie had signed the lease papers almost two weeks ago, Edgar had given her free rein to transform the interior of the building – on her dime, of course – so she'd contracted with Andy's construction company to take care of the necessary renovations. They'd been at work since Edgar handed over the keys on Monday.

"I'm calling because we came across something while we were tearing out the old drywall, and I thought you'd want to know about it." He paused, waiting for her response.

Her blood ran cold. She'd seen her share of reality TV remodeling shows. It was never a good sign to have your contractor call you out of the blue with news about finding something. What could it possibly be? An issue with removing the wall? Termites?

She wasn't sure she wanted to know. The ink was barely dry on the lease, and she was already running into problems. Although she was fairly certain she wasn't responsible for termites, any issues could put her behind schedule, and she needed to get the bakery up and running as quickly as possible.

"What did you find?" She gripped the phone, her gaze straying to the remodeling budget line on her spreadsheet. How much was this going to cost her?

He cleared his throat. "It's the strangest thing. One of my men pulled out a chunk of the wall across from the counter and found a mural or something behind it."

Her heart beat faster. "A mural?"

"Yeah. It looks like someone painted the ocean and coastline on the original wall." He laughed. "It's pretty good, actually. I think it might be really old, so we thought you should take a look at it before we finish removing the drywall."

Cassie stood from her chair and paced the length of the kitchen floor. The kids would be home soon, but this sounded like something she needed to take care of immediately or the workers wouldn't be able to continue. "Okay. I'll be there in about half an hour. Thanks for letting me know about it."

"See you then." Andy hung up.

Cassie dialed her next-door neighbor, Kim. Their daughters were best friends and they often traded babysitting.

"Hey, Kim. It's Cassie."

"Hi, Cassie," Kim answered. "How are you doing?"

"I'm doing great." Cassie saved her spreadsheet and shut the lid on her laptop. "I had something come up at the bakery, and I was wondering if you could watch my kids for about an hour or so."

Kim's voice was warm. "Of course. That's no problem. Cammie will be thrilled to have Amanda over. Do you want me to get them as soon as they get home?"

"If you could wait for them outside, that would be great," Cassie said. "I don't want them to find the front door locked and be worried."

"I'll head out now. They should be here soon."

"Thank you so much." Cassie sighed. "I owe you." She had a sinking feeling that this may become an all too common occurrence now that she was a full-time business owner. At least they lived within walking distance of the bakery. If she needed to be there while they weren't in school, the kids could hang out in a back room and do their homework.

Kim laughed. "You can pay me back with a treat from the bakery. Donny and I were just talking about going to your grand opening. We're both so excited for you."

"Thank you. I really appreciate all of your help."

"You're very welcome." The sound of an exterior door shutting carried over the phone line, and Kim said, "I see them coming down the street. I'll go grab them."

"Thanks again." Cassie hung up the phone, then grabbed her house keys and wallet.

She walked briskly out the back door of the house and cut the few blocks over to Main Street. By the time she reached the bakery, she was breathing hard from the exertion of speed walking. She'd been thinking about making exercise more of a priority, but with everything she had going on, it had fallen by the wayside. Ironically, instead of focusing on her health, she'd bought a bakery, where she'd constantly be surrounded by the tantalizing aroma of breads and pastries.

All of the tables in front of the bakery had been pushed against the building. The umbrellas were missing, but Edgar had told her that he'd put them in a small storage shed at the rear of the property. A closed sign hung on the glass pane of the front door, and the flyers that had once papered the front windows had been removed.

She pushed in the door, her stomach fluttering. The smell of bread hung in the air, although it had been at least five days since anything had baked in there. All of the inside tables had been moved to the back room in preparation for the renovations to the main customer area.

Behind the counter to the left, two men were working on installing new electrical outlets. Andy stood in front of her to the right, peering into a three-by-three-foot gap in the wall. Thick white dust particles covered the floor below it, and the discarded chunks of Sheetrock lay in a pile a few feet away.

He backed up and greeted her when he heard the door. "Hi, Cassie. Thanks for coming down to see this."

She nodded. "No problem. I have to admit, I'm pretty curious to see what you've found."

He gestured to her to stand beside him. "You can see part of it, but it looks like it might extend at least a few feet in either direction." He aimed the beam of a small flashlight into the hole, illuminating a stretch of blue and green paint between the studs framing the wall. "I think they may have built out the wall at some point, but they didn't want to ruin the painting." He moved aside to allow her room to see the uncovered portion of the mural.

She stepped back to assess the visible parts of the image and sucked in her breath. The blues, greens, and browns took the shape of waves breaking upon a rocky arm of land reaching out past a sandy shoreline. Even in this small portion of the painting, Cassie could see the artist had captured the essence of California's central coastline.

Memories of Monterey flooded her brain, and she blinked back tears.

"Are you okay?" Andy asked.

She rubbed at her eyes, but couldn't contain her emotions. "Yeah. I think I got some dust in my eye, though. I'm going to head to the bathroom to try to wash it out."

He nodded. "Let me know if you need anything." He tipped his head toward the mural. "Is it okay if I take off some more of this drywall? I'll do my best not to damage the painting, but I think it should be fine with the way they framed this wall."

"That's fine." She hurried to the bathroom and locked the door behind her. Edgar had left the bathroom sparkling clean, and she sat down for a minute on the lid of the toilet seat to think.

Over a decade ago, Cassie and Kyle had spent seven magical days and nights honeymooning in the Monterey Bay area of California. They hadn't been able to afford anything fancy, but had lucked out with an ocean-view room in an old hotel tucked into a rocky point amongst the dunes. It was being updated by new owners, so the lobby had been in a state of disarray, but Cassie and Kyle couldn't have cared less. They spent their days exploring the charming towns and beaches dotting the coast between Monterey and Big Sur, and their evenings experiencing the amazing cuisine of the local restaurants. In those days, Cassie couldn't have ever imagined a life apart from Kyle.

Someone tapped on the door. "Are you okay in there?" Andy asked.

She plucked a wad of toilet paper off the roll and dabbed at her eyes. "I'm fine. I'll be out in a minute."

Through the closed door, she heard his footsteps recede as he walked away. She blew her nose and threw the toilet paper into the garbage, then washed her hands at the sink and stared into the mirror.

Was being divorced ever going to get easier? Was it normal to feel so emotional years after a marriage had ended? Maybe it was just because they had kids and still had a connection. If it had been a clean split, Kyle would be out of her life, and she wouldn't be thinking about him at all. But even time couldn't erase her memories of all of the special moments they'd had together.

In her reflection, her lips quivered, but she pushed them together, forming fine lines on her cheeks. Her skin was pink from crying, so she pulled her hair back from her face and splashed it with water. After drying off with a rough paper towel, she blinked a few times at her image and rolled her shoulders back. This wasn't the time or place to focus on her failed marriage. She had a business to run.

When she emerged from the back of the bakery, Andy

had his crew removing small sections of the wall at a time, and a few more feet of mural had already been exposed. Cassie glanced at the painting, but didn't look at it too closely for fear of turning on the waterworks again.

"How long do you think it's been there?" she asked Andy.

He shrugged. "No idea. It looks old, but you never know. I would guess before Edgar turned the space into a bakery, though."

"This has been a bakery since we were kids," Cassie said. "I don't remember it ever being anything else."

"Me neither." He stared at the image. "So, it must have been one of the previous tenants. You could ask Edgar."

"I will, but I don't want to interrupt him right now. He and his wife left on a house-hunting mission to Arizona the day after he turned the bakery over to me." She eyed the artwork. "Do you think anyone else in town might know?"

Andy shoved his hands into his jeans pockets and looked up at the ceiling, his face contorted with thought. His lips slid into a smile and he said, "You know, you might check with Chase at the art gallery. I've heard he's into local art."

"Is that the new owner?" Cassie asked.

Andy raised an eyebrow and laughed. "The new owner?"

She smirked at him. "You know what I mean. The guy who bought it from Linda Canter." The art gallery had changed hands about a year ago, but Cassie hadn't visited the business for ages.

He laughed again. "Yeah. Chase Flaherty is his name. He's a good guy. We did some construction work for him."

She checked her watch. "The gallery should be open for a while longer. I'll take a picture once your guys are done pulling off the drywall and take it over to him." At the rate the construction workers were moving, they would be done soon.

He nodded. "You should probably give some thought to what you want to do with the wall. If we can't easily remove the mural panels, we'll have to tear them out to put in that eating counter you wanted."

She sighed. "Yeah, I was afraid of that." She looked at the progress so far. The painted expanse was growing, and it was likely that the mural covered the entire length of the wall. "Let's hold off on making any decisions until I find out more about it."

"Sounds like a good plan. I'll let the guys know." He walked over to the two workers and conferred with them, then started helping them tear away the drywall.

After about an hour, the demolition project was complete. They all stood about ten feet back from the mural to take it in. Cassie suppressed any emotions that arose and attempted to look at it objectively. It was a gorgeous representation of the best facets of the Monterey Peninsula. One panel in particular tugged at Cassie's heartstrings – a man and a woman sitting together on a bench, gazing out at the ocean.

She swallowed hard and made herself snap a few photos of the mural with her camera phone while the others continued viewing the masterpiece.

"I've never seen anything like it," one of the men said.

"Me neither," said another. "I've been in the business for thirty years, and I've never come across something like this."

Andy smiled at Cassie. "Looks like you've got a centerpiece wall."

She laughed. "Yeah, but it's not the bar I wanted." She

zoomed in to focus on the couple on the bench – to show Chase, of course.

"I'm sure we can figure out a different layout if you want to keep this in the bakery." Andy walked over to the wall and lightly ran his hand over the paint. "I have to admit I'm extremely curious to find out who did this and why it was walled over."

She held up her phone, one of the photos she'd just taken showing on the screen. "Well, I'm going to see if I can find out. I'll let you know if I discover anything."

"Thanks." He grinned at her. "We'll probably be gone when you're done at the gallery, but give me a call and let me know how you want to proceed."

"Will do. Have a nice evening." She shoved her phone into her pocket.

"You too." Andy grabbed a broom from the corner and began sweeping up the construction mess as she exited the bakery.

The art gallery was only a few blocks down Main Street, but it took Cassie about ten minutes to navigate through the crowds. The sidewalks were packed with tourists on their way to an early dinner or ducking into shops to buy souvenirs. By the time she reached the gallery, it was a few minutes after five o'clock, but the sign on the door still read Open.

She turned the doorknob and pushed on the door, stepping onto a gleaming hardwood floor. The gallery had changed quite a bit from when she was last there. Under the former owner, the space had been cozy. Now, stark white walls allowed the art to provide all of the color in the room, and glass display cases sprouted up like stalagmites rising from the floor of a cavern.

A few people were examining paintings on the wall. One customer stood in front of a tall counter in the corner while a man who could easily have been a fashion model carefully wrapped a small object in tissue and set it in a white paper box. When the customer left with his purchase, Cassie approached the counter.

"Hi," she said. "I'm hoping to speak with the owner about a painting I found recently."

The man looked up at her, his eyes sparkling in a face too handsome for comfort. "Well, I'd love to hear about this painting." He came around to the front of the desk and held out his hand. "I'm Chase Flaherty, and this is my gallery."

She shook his hand. Heat radiated from his fingers as they wrapped around hers for a few moments longer than necessary. "Cassie Thorsen. Nice to meet you."

"So, tell me about this painting," he said.

"Well, actually, it's a huge mural." She turned to gesture in the direction she'd come from. "I recently took over Edgar's Bakery, and during renovations the workers uncovered a mural behind some drywall."

He looked in the direction she was pointing. "Edgar's is in that old Spanish Mediterranean Revival building down on Fifth Street, right?"

"That's the one." She peered at him. "Why? Are you familiar with the building?" Excitement built in her chest. Did he know anything about the artist?

He laughed. "I know where it's at, but that's about it. Do you want me to go over there later today to see the mural?"

"Actually, I took a few photos of it." Cassie looked around the gallery, which was now almost empty. "Do you have time now to look at them?" She met his gaze, hoping that he would. She held her phone out to him.

"Sure. That's fine." He leaned against the counter and took the phone from her, scrolling through the photos she'd taken. He went past the last image of the mural and paused on a picture of Jace and Amanda that she'd taken at the beach. "Cute kids."

Her face flushed. "Thanks." She swiped her finger across the phone screen to bring it back to the mural. "Do you recognize the artwork?"

He used his thumb and forefinger to zoom in on some of the details. "It looks familiar, but I couldn't say for sure. Let me make some calls tonight, and I'll get back to you. Would you be willing to text me the photos?"

"Oh, yeah, sure." Cassie reached for the phone, almost fumbling it when his hand touched hers. She attached the images to a text message, then asked, "What's your phone number?"

He rattled off the digits, and she entered them, then hit send. From behind the counter came a loud ding.

"I guess you got them." She winced, wishing she hadn't said such an inane thing. He must think she was an idiot.

He walked over to his phone and tapped on the screen. "Yep. Thanks."

"If you want to see it in person, just let me know. The bakery isn't open yet, but I can let you in to view it."

The door closed behind the last potential customer in the gallery. Chase watched the door swing shut. "I could see it now. I usually close up about five on the weekdays, depending on how busy we are." When she checked her watch, he said, "I'm sorry, I shouldn't have asked. You have kids and a husband to get home to."

By now, her cheeks were probably as pink as the

button-down blouse she was wearing. "Actually, I'm divorced, but I should get back to my kids. They're with my neighbor right now. Would tomorrow afternoon at two thirty work?"

He smiled. "My assistant will be here tomorrow, so I can play hooky for a while. I'll meet you there, and I'll ask around about the mural tonight."

"Thanks. I really appreciate it." Cassie looked around the gallery. "You've done a great job with this place. I don't remember it seeming quite so spacious before."

He beamed. "That's because I moved some walls around when I bought the building. It used to be a bunch of cramped little rooms, but I wanted the space opened up to better the flow."

"Well, it's a great change." Cassie smiled at him. "I'll see you tomorrow."

"It was nice meeting you, Cassie." He reached out and touched her arm.

"Nice meeting you too."

She walked directly home from the art gallery, her thoughts a confusing mixture of awe over the beautiful mural they'd uncovered, memories of her honeymoon with Kyle in Monterey, and meeting Chase. She was somewhat surprised she'd never met him before, but she was usually locked up at the Lodge during the day and home with her kids in the evening. That left little time for socializing around town. Like Andy had said, Chase seemed like a great guy, although she wasn't sure how she felt about his flirty behavior. He probably was like that with everyone, but it had been a while since anyone had flirted with her, and she found it disconcerting.

12

Libby

Libby dropped Kaya off at her mom's house and got back into the car. For a minute, she sat there, just staring at her hands on the steering wheel. Her mom had offered to take Kaya during the day and would be picking up the rest of the kids after school. Libby had a whole day to herself, something that hadn't happened in a long time. Now the only question was, what was she going to do?

Her brain filled with images of the overflowing piles of laundry that were an everyday occurrence with four kids in the house, the sticky kitchen floor, and the dog hair that had accumulated on the couch. She turned the key in the ignition and started driving home, then caught herself. Did she really want to waste this free day on chores?

She pulled over to the side of the road and took a good look at her reflection in the rearview mirror. A woman in her mid-thirties with dark circles under her eyes and long, stringy brown hair stared back at her. When she'd been younger, she'd always taken pride in her appearance, but that had changed as the kids occupied more and more of her time. A sharp pain stabbed at her chest, and her breath hitched. Was that why Gabe had lost interest in her? Was he no longer attracted to her?

Libby ran her fingers through her hair, examining the split ends made visible by the sunlight. It hadn't been cut in over a year. Come to think of it, she couldn't remember the last time she'd taken any time out for herself. Before she could change her mind, she called her hairdresser and made an appointment, leaving just enough time beforehand for a trip to Wedding Belles for an indulgent dark chocolate mocha.

By the time she walked out of the hair salon just off Main Street, she was feeling more human. She strolled down the main drag in Willa Bay, taking the time to window-shop and savor the warmth of the summer day.

When she walked past what used to be Edgar's Bakery, she stopped. A closed sign hung in the window, but the lights were on. She cupped her hands against the window to keep the glare away, and peered inside.

Cassie sat at a small table in the middle of the room. Nearby, two men were reconstructing a counter. Should she bother her friend? Libby made a quick decision and pushed on the door. It swung open easily, and she stepped inside.

Cassie's head popped up at the intrusion, but her lips spread into a wide smile when she saw who had entered. "Hey, Libby."

"Hey." Libby looked around. "Wow. I can't believe how different it looks in here." The last time she'd been inside Edgar's, it had been filled with people, and she could barely see the tiled floor. The space appeared five times larger now, especially with the different counter.

Cassie laughed. "We've barely done anything yet. Wait until you see it after it's all in place and painted."

"Speaking of paint." Libby pointed at a mural spanning the entire wall. She'd never seen anything quite like it indoors. "Where did that come from? Was it here all along?"

Cassie nodded. "They found it yesterday while removing the drywall. Can you believe that was underneath?"

Libby walked closer to the painting. From far away, it was beautiful, but from only a foot away, it was stunning. The artist had included small details that made the artwork come to life, like wispy strands of grass on the top of the dunes. "Wow."

"I know." Cassie moved across the room to stand quietly by Libby's side. "Every time I look at it, I see something I hadn't noticed before."

Libby scanned the length of the painting. "It looks like the California coast." She swallowed a lump in her throat. Visiting that area with Gabe had always been on her bucket list. The way things were going with him, though, there wasn't much chance of that ever happening.

"That's what I'm guessing. I think it's the Monterey Peninsula – at least how I remember it." A far-off look came into Cassie's eyes before she cast her gaze down at her shoes, tracing a line in the fine dust coating the floor below the mural.

"Do you know who painted it?" Libby walked along the mural to view the rest of it up-close.

Cassie shrugged. "Not yet. I talked to Chase, the new owner of the art gallery, but he didn't know off the top of his head. He said he'd ask around about it, so I sent him photos that he could share with some of his contacts."

"So, he might be able to find out who the artist is?"

Libby stepped back again to take in the whole thing. The artist's passion for their subject came through in every square inch of the panels. "It's like you got a mystery along with your bakery."

"I know." Cassie smiled. "I wasn't sure when I saw it for the first time yesterday, but the idea of keeping it is growing on me." She nodded to the notebook lying on the small table she'd been sitting at. "I was planning on making this wall into a counter to eat at, but I think I'm going to change things around so I can keep the mural." She touched the wall with a gentle finger. "I really hope I find out who created this. Chase is coming over in an hour to tell me what he's discovered from his contacts." She blushed when she said his name.

Libby grinned. When they'd shown out-of-town guests around town last year, she'd visited the art gallery. Its proprietor was one of the most handsome men she'd ever seen, and Cassie didn't seem to be immune to his charms. Her friend had been hurting since her marriage had ended several years ago, and it was about time she started dating again.

"What did you think of Chase?" Libby asked innocently.

Cassie turned an even darker shade of pink. "He was nice."

"Nice?" Libby teased. "Is that all you noticed about him?" Prying into her friend's love life was much more fun than worrying about the problems in her own marriage.

"Okay, he was good-looking too." Cassie mock-glared at Libby. "Have you met him before?"

She nodded. "Once. I don't buy a lot of art, but we had friends that wanted to go in there while they were in town." Libby walked over to the table Cassie had been working at and picked up a drawing of what looked to be an interior design schematic. "Is this the bakery?"

"Yeah. I'm trying to figure out what to do now that I don't have my eating counter." Cassie took the paper from her and scrutinized it. She frowned. "I can't seem to make it work, but I'd really like to keep the mural."

"Do you mind if I take a look?" Libby asked. "I studied interior design in college."

Cassie shrugged. "Sure. I'd be happy to have some help."

They pored over the plans together, eventually making some minor rearrangements to the layout.

"Did you make any decisions about the mural?" a man asked.

Libby and Cassie looked up to see Andy Avery standing in front of them. They'd all grown up together, and it hadn't come as a surprise to anyone in town when Andy had started his own construction company. He'd always been building something when they were kids. In fact, Libby's own parents still had a few of his birdhouses in their backyard.

Libby smiled at him. "Hi, Andy."

"Hey, Libby," he said. "What do you think of the mural we found?"

"It's pretty amazing." She gazed at the painting. "I can't believe it's been covered up all these years."

"No kidding." He grinned. "I'm kind of hoping Cassie decides to keep it."

"Well, I definitely want to keep it." Cassie held up the piece of paper. "What do you think about this layout? Is it doable?"

He accepted the paper and scanned it for a moment. "This should work. I'll let the guys know."

"Thanks," Cassie said. "How much longer do you think it'll take to complete the project?"

He stuck his thumbs in the front pockets of his jeans and gazed at the ceiling with his face contorted with thought. "Maybe another week? We still need to finish the counter, add in the bar, and then install the flooring."

"Great." Cassie shook her head in disbelief. "I can't believe this is moving along so fast."

Andy puffed up a little. "We work fast."

Cassie laughed, but worry clouded her face. "I meant that, a month ago, owning a bakery was the furthest thing from my mind. Now I'll be opening within a few weeks." She patted his arm. "But I do appreciate how hard you and your crew have been working."

He smiled. "Of course. I'm happy to help. And you're going to do great." He looked over his shoulder at the men working on the counter. "Speaking of construction deadlines, I'd better get back to work." He glanced at Libby. "Nice seeing you again."

"You too," she said. Andy walked away, and Libby peered at Cassie. "How are you doing? You seem a little overwhelmed."

Cassie took a deep breath and her shoulders slumped as she leaned back in her chair. "I am, a little." Her eyes roamed over the bakery. "I can't believe this place is mine now. It's a lot of responsibility."

Libby reached across the table and squeezed Cassie's hand. "You're ready for it. I can't even tell you how many times I've heard people raving about your custom cakes or the treats you make for the Willa Bay Lodge." She gestured to the construction mess. "When this is all cleaned up, people are going to flock to your bakery, just like they did when it was Edgar's."

Cassie's spine straightened, and a glimmer of a smile

came over her lips. "Thanks." She eyed Libby. "When you and your mom started your catering business, did you ever worry?"

Libby chuckled. "Of course we did. We still do. Over the years, we've managed to gain a reputation in town for providing excellent food at a good value, but it hasn't been easy. We had to work hard to get there. And when Mom was sick last year, we cut back a lot, so we lost some ground."

Her chest constricted, thinking of her mother's cancer diagnosis and treatment. It had been worth taking time off from the business to allow her mom time to heal from her surgery and chemotherapy, but their finances and client list had taken a hit. Libby had come to depend on her income from their catering company, so the last two years had been rough. She and Gabe had dipped into their savings quite a bit to make ends meet, but they'd managed.

She and her mom had increased their bookings over the last month, but business still wasn't at the level they'd been at before. With the state of her marriage so uncertain, Libby needed that income. She didn't want to be caught unprepared if they ever separated. Libby stared out the window, her eyes glazing over. How had their relationship gotten so bad that she was considering what to do if he wasn't in the picture?

"Libby?" Cassie asked. "You okay?"

Libby blinked a few times to moisten her eyes. "I'm fine. Just thinking a little."

Cassie scooted her chair closer. "What's going on? How is your mom?"

Libby gave her a small smile. "Mom's fine. She's as healthy as a horse now." She twisted her fingers in her lap. "It's Gabe."

Cassie stared at her. "What's going on with Gabe?"

"He's been so distant lately, staying late at work and snapping at me whenever we do talk." Libby sniffed, hoping to hold back the tears that threatened to erupt. Airing her dirty laundry didn't come naturally to her, but her sisters hadn't been around to confide in lately. If she didn't talk to someone about it soon, she worried she would explode the next time she saw her husband.

"Has he said anything to you?" Cassie asked.

Libby snorted. "Like that he's having an affair or something?"

Cassie's eyes widened. "He's having an affair?" she whispered.

"No." Libby sighed. "At least, not that I know of. But something is wrong."

"Have you talked to him about it?"

Libby shook her head. "I've tried to, but he always shuts me down and says nothing is wrong." She rested her elbows on the table and dropped her head into her hands. Her freshly cut and washed hair cascaded around her face like a curtain she could hide behind.

"I'm sorry, Libs," Cassie said.

Libby looked up. "Thanks." She had a hard time keeping her voice from trembling, and she didn't like the way that made her feel. She'd always taken pride in staying calm and collected, even in the face of adversity. Unfortunately, she'd never expected adversity to come from within her own marriage. Until this past year, she would have described her relationship with Gabe as rock solid. Now it was about as solid as the cherry Jell-O she'd made for dessert last night.

"You've got to talk with him," Cassie said.

"I know." Libby balled her hands into fists, then flexed her fingers. "But I can't make him talk to me."

"You have to." Cassie pressed her lips together, and a pained expression crossed her face. "Don't let things go for so long that they can't be fixed."

Her words tugged at Libby's heart. She studied her friend. "Do you ever wish you'd tried harder with Kyle?"

"Every day," Cassie said in a voice so low that Libby strained to hear it. Cassie took a deep breath and smoothed her hair back from her face. "But I can't change my past. You still have time with Gabe. Talk to him, Libby. Find out what's bothering him."

"But what if I don't like what I find out?" Libby's heart twisted. She *had* tried to talk to Gabe, but had she tried hard enough? Did she really want to know what was going on with him, or was it better not to know?

If she never heard the truth from him, maybe she could pretend that nothing was wrong. She pushed her chair back from the table and stood. Since when had she ever backed down from anything in her life?

The doorbell jingled and Chase Flaherty entered. He looked between Cassie and Libby. "Am I interrupting something?"

"No, no." Libby forced a smile to her lips. "Actually, I was just leaving." She held out her hand. "You probably don't remember me, but I'm Libby Briggs Jansen. We met once, about a year ago."

"Of course I know who you are." He flashed her a toothy grin. "Everyone in town knows the Briggs family."

She laughed, more at ease now. "Well, I wouldn't say *everyone*. But, it's nice to see you again. Are you here about the mural?"

"I am." He looked over at Cassie, eyeing her appraisingly.

Behind his back, Libby winked at Cassie. "He's cute," she mouthed.

Cassie shook her head slightly and got up from the table. "Thanks for coming over here. Did you find anything out about the artist?"

"No, not yet. But I've got some feelers out." He motioned to the mural. "Do you mind if I take a look?"

Cassie shrugged. "Be my guest." She and Chase walked over to the wall, and Libby followed a few steps behind. With the kids at her parents' house for the night, Libby had plenty of time before she needed to get home to make dinner for Gabe, and she was intensely curious about the provenance of the mural.

"It's even more spectacular than the photos you showed me." He moved closer to the painting and scrutinized it. "Have you seen a signature on it?"

"No, but I definitely could have missed one because it covers such a large area. It must have taken the artist a year or more to paint it."

"Most likely." Chase slowly moved down the wall. In the far corner, he halted and dropped to a crouch, then pointed at a faint scribble of brown paint that was almost concealed in the corner of a panel. "Look at that!"

Cassie and Libby crowded around him.

"It's a signature, isn't it?" Cassie asked.

Chase beamed at her. "Sure looks like it." He took out his phone and snapped a shot of the text before standing upright to view the image on the phone screen. Zooming in made the signature clearer, but Libby still couldn't read it.

"Do you recognize it?" Libby asked.

He shook his head. "No." He peered at the screen. "I can't quite make it out, but I'll keep trying to decipher it." They moved a comfortable distance apart, but Chase kept staring at the signature. "I swear I've seen this before."

"Really?" Cassie's face lit up.

His brow furrowed. "Yes, but I can't think of where I saw it. It'll come to me, though." He turned to face Cassie directly. "I'd better get back to the gallery, but I'll let you know as soon as I find out anything. Maybe we can get together over coffee sometime to discuss it?"

Cassie coughed suddenly and couldn't seem to get her words out, so Libby stepped in before her friend could embarrass herself further. "That would be great. Thank you for helping Cassie with this. I know she appreciates your help and would love to discuss the mural with you later." She looked at Cassie meaningfully.

Cassie nodded, finally able to speak. "Yes, thank you."

He raised an eyebrow. "I'll talk to you later then." He touched Cassie's arm, then gave Libby a little wave. "Nice meeting you." With a quick pivot, he strode out the door.

Libby turned to Cassie. "I think he likes you. He was flirting with you."

Cassie looked a little green. "I'm sure he flirts with everyone."

"No, that was definitely aimed at you." Libby grinned. "He even asked you to coffee."

"To discuss the mural, I'm sure." Cassie made a show of checking her watch. "I'd better be getting home. The kids will be there soon. Don't you need to get home too?"

"No, Mom is watching them tonight." Libby spread her arms out wide. "I'm a free woman today."

Cassie sighed. "Must be nice to have your parents living so close. My parents only see the kids about once a month and it's the same for Kyle's parents."

"It is nice," Libby admitted. "But they don't usually want to take all four kids at the same time."

They said goodbye to Andy and the work crew, then walked outside onto the sunlit sidewalk.

"I'll see you on the Fourth of July, right?" Cassie asked. "If not sooner, that is."

"Yep, we wouldn't miss it," Libby said. Her whole family went every year to the big Willa Bay fireworks show and celebration at the park by the water. It was an annual tradition they all enjoyed, and it usually involved a big picnic on the beach. Gabe always loved cooking hot dogs for lunch over a barbecue pit at the park. She bit her lip. Would he even be there this year?

"Great, I'll see you then." Cassie gave Libby a hug and said into her ear so no passersby could hear, "And I'm sure everything with Gabe will work out."

Libby nodded, but a chill ran through her body. "I hope so."

Cassie jetted off down the street, and Libby walked back to the other end of Main Street where she'd parked her car. Today had been a nice diversion, but she needed to get back to real life, or at least part of it. The kids may be with her parents for the night, but Gabe would be coming home for dinner, and she intended to make him listen to her concerns.

Three hours later, Libby slumped into an armchair in their living room, staring into the kitchen. The table was set for two, but the shrimp and asparagus risotto she'd carefully arranged in shallow bowls had long ago turned into a congealed mush. She'd spent over an hour making Gabe's favorite meal, and he hadn't even bothered to call to let her know he'd be late. At this point, she didn't even know if he planned to come home.

A tear slipped down her cheek, followed by dozens more. She wanted Gabe in her life, but at this rate, they were never going to take that dream trip together to Monterey. How could she fix her relationship if he wasn't even there?

13

Meg

Meg stared at the Inn's half-renovated kitchen. A granite countertop leaned against the wall, the new farmhouse sink on the plywood floor next to it. "I thought this was supposed to be done by now."

"Well, it's not," Zoe snapped back at her. She ran both hands over her scalp, threading her fingers through her hair and tugging on it gently. "Argh! Nothing is going right."

"At least they were able to fix the water damage. Who knows when that leak started. It's lucky we remodeled the kitchen now before it got too bad," Meg said. They'd lost about a week's worth of time to contain the mold and rot behind the sink, but now the kitchen remodel could go forward.

"Yeah, lucky." Zoe scowled. "Between this and the roofers bailing on us, we're so far behind schedule that it's not even funny."

"I wasn't laughing." Meg crossed her arms.

"Maybe not, but you don't have to deal with it." Zoe's eyes were weary as she surveyed the kitchen.

"I'm here as much as possible," Meg said.

"Yeah. But it's not enough. How is it that you have time to go out with that new boyfriend of yours, but not help us here?"

Meg recoiled. She'd been out with Theo a few times over the last two weeks, but it wasn't like she saw him every day. His lighthearted attitude made him fun to be around and took her mind off the long hours she devoted to work and the Inn.

"We both agreed that I'd keep my job for a few more months." Meg tried to keep her voice even, but heat was rising in her chest as her temper threatened to get the better of her. Zoe was stressed to the max, but that didn't mean she had the right to take it out on Meg. If this was what it was like being in business with one of her closest friends, she wasn't sure if it was worth it.

"You wanted to keep your job." Zoe sighed. "Look I don't want to fight about this. I just want things to go right."

Meg met Zoe's gaze. "I know. Me too. Seriously, we're all in this together – you, me, and Shawn."

"I know." Zoe appeared to have aged several years over the last two months. "It's just not how I thought it would be."

Meg's heart softened, and she wrapped her arms around Zoe, patting her on the back. "It'll get better."

"Thanks." Zoe looked up to the ceiling. "I keep waiting for the other shoe to drop, though. What next? A sinkhole develops in the driveway? A raging rhino knocks over the new gazebo?"

Meg smirked. "Those are probably unlikely."

In the hallway outside of the kitchen, the tennis balls

on the back of Celia's walker clopped rhythmically on the hardwood floors, and she appeared in the entrance to the kitchen. She looked sharply between the two of them. "Are you girls all right?"

"We're fine." Zoe gave her a tight-lipped smile. "Just wondering what else can go wrong."

Celia smiled. "On that note, I do have some news for you. I'm not sure if you'll consider it good or bad."

Meg narrowed her eyes at the elderly woman. "What is it?" If it was an escaped rhino, she was moving back to Portland.

"Bruce Danville skipped town, along with all of the deposits people had paid for their events at Danville Hall." Celia frowned. "I never did trust that guy."

Meg and Zoe exchanged worried glances.

"What do you mean, skipped town?" Zoe asked.

"So, what happens with the scheduled events?" Meg asked.

Celia shook her head. "I don't know. From what I heard, the employees found a sign on the door this morning that Danville Hall had closed. They're still trying to figure out what's going on, but, apparently, Bruce emptied the business accounts before leaving on a one-way ticket to Mexico this morning."

"All of those weddings," Zoe whispered, her eyes wide with shock. "How awful."

"I know." Celia came all the way into the kitchen and sat down on the only chair remaining in the torn up room. "I'm sure they were fully booked for the summer and fall – they always are."

"Why would he do that?" Meg asked.

"Who knows," Celia shrugged. "But clients paid him huge deposits to secure their reservations and now they've lost both that money and the venue."

Zoe looked around the room. "I wish we could do something to help, but we don't open until late August. Maybe we could run a special discount for people who were supposed to have their events at Danville Hall?"

Meg took a deep breath. "I know this is a long shot, but is there any chance we could open early? Like maybe at the beginning of August? That could help a lot of people."

A far-off look came into Zoe's eyes, and Meg knew she was reviewing her to-do list and calculating how much time everything would take.

"Maybe?" Zoe said. "But we'd have to find a roofing company that can start in the next two weeks. We can't proceed with the upstairs renovations until we get the roof fixed."

"Okay, but if we can make that happen, can we do it?" Meg asked.

"It'll be close, but maybe?" Zoe didn't look too certain of her assessment. "I'd love to help all of those people because they've been put into a horrible situation. I can't imagine inviting hundreds of people to my wedding and then finding out a week beforehand that the venue no longer exists. Plus, Danville Hall required that clients use their in-house caterers and florist, so they'd have to find those services as well."

"Wouldn't we have to do that too?" Meg asked.

"Yeah, but I can find people for that." Zoe grinned. "Over the last decade in this business, I've made more than a few contacts I can count on. If the vendors that were going to provide services to Danville Hall events were left in the lurch, too, they're probably available." She toed the edge of a scrap of linoleum that stuck stubbornly to the plywood floor and looked over at Celia. "What do you think?"

Celia leaned against her walker, taking time to compose her thoughts before speaking. "I think we can make it happen by the beginning of August. And I might have an idea for the roof. I've been thinking about it, and I may know some people who owe me a favor."

Meg smiled. Zoe may have been involved with Willa Bay's wedding industry for a decade, but Celia had about half a century more experience with it. She had no doubt that Celia could pull off any event she wanted to on a moment's notice.

Meg raised her eyebrows and locked eyes with Zoe, who smiled back at her.

"I guess we're going to do this," Zoe said. "I'll tell Shawn that, somehow, we'll open by the beginning of August. The Inn may not be in top form, but we'll make sure that any client-facing areas are ready. Celia, can you let people know we'd be happy to help out clients of Danville Hall?"

Celia nodded. "I'll check with the Chamber of Commerce to find out if anyone is coordinating efforts to find new venues for them."

Meg checked her watch. Her shift at the Lodge was about to start.

"Meg, can you help me decide what to prioritize before we open?" Zoe asked.

Meg froze. Zoe was already upset with her and she hated to let her down yet again. "I'm so sorry, but I have to go to work now."

Zoe's face fell. "Oh."

"I can come back tomorrow morning, though," she said, ignoring the sinking feeling in her chest. She'd planned on spending the morning running errands and tidying her apartment, which had been sorely neglected lately.

Zoe sighed. "I guess that will have to do." She turned to Celia. "Can you find out if you can get a roofer out here soon?"

"I'll do it before I call the Chamber of Commerce." Celia smiled at Zoe. "Don't worry, dear. It'll all work out."

"I sure hope so." Zoe didn't look too certain.

Meg clocked into work and started preparing for dinner, but couldn't focus. Her head ached from worrying about Zoe's feelings, and her muscles burned from all of the physical labor she'd done recently at the Inn. She rolled her shoulders back, wincing as the muscles around her shoulder blades lengthened and contracted.

"Are you okay?" Taylor asked as he came around the side of the counter island. "You look like you got run over by a truck." His eyes widened and he stumbled to correct himself. "That's not what I meant. It's just that you look like you're hurting."

She laughed. "No offense taken. I *am* in pain." She braced her hands against the counter and leaned back, stretching out her forearms. "I've been helping Zoe paint and do about a million other things at the Inn." She frowned, remembering how upset Zoe had been with her earlier. "But none of that seems to be enough for her."

"I'm sure she knows how hard you're trying." Taylor peered at her, leaning one hip against the counter and folding his arms in front of him. "You're doing everything you can."

"She doesn't seem to think so." Meg reached for the knife on the counter. Zoe hadn't been happy that Meg had been spending time with Theo, and her accusations had stung, but maybe she had a point. Meg had considered calling Theo on her way to work to talk about it, but she'd decided against it. While Theo was fun to be around and she was enjoying her time with him, they weren't at the place yet where she could unload everything that was on her mind. That kind of relationship was built over time. But, Zoe probably had free time to spend with Shawn, right? Why shouldn't Meg have the same opportunities for fun?

However, this didn't seem appropriate to share with Taylor. Meg hadn't told him she was dating someone and it hadn't come up in conversation. If Cassie was right about him having feelings for her, she didn't want to hurt him inadvertently.

She put the knife down. "For some reason, I had this crazy idea that I'd love being in business with Zoe. I'd always admired her work ethic here, and she's so organized and on top of things. I thought with her in charge, renovating the Inn would be a breeze. What I didn't consider was how she gets when things don't go according to plan. And with the Inn, *nothing* is following the approved timeline."

He nodded slowly. "But that's not your fault."

"No, but I think Zoe is looking for anyone to blame." She sighed. "That's not really fair. She's taken on a huge responsibility, and I don't think it's exactly how she envisioned things going either." Her eyes blurred with unshed tears.

He came over and put an arm around her, drawing her close to his chest. Her body went stiff for a few seconds, but then she relaxed against him. Taylor had a way of calming her and making her believe that things would be okay. She'd never found that with anyone else, including the few boyfriends she'd had over the years. When she eventually quit her job at the Lodge, she'd miss him and his support.

"Am I interrupting something?" Lara's voice cut through Meg's bubble of safety, and she sprang away from Taylor, wiping her eyes with the back of her hand.

"Nope," Meg said.

Taylor eyed Lara with disdain and walked into his office, closing the door. Cassie only had one more day at the Lodge before she left to work full-time at her new bakery. Of course, as soon as Cassie had announced her resignation, Lara had been named her replacement and started her on-the-job training the week before. Meg wasn't looking forward to working with Lara on a daily basis, especially with her two best friends defecting from the Lodge.

Lara looked around the room. "I'm definitely going to need to make some changes when I take over from Cassie. This place isn't arranged very efficiently."

Raged seethed under Meg's skin. "That's because most of it is set up for a restaurant kitchen's workflow."

"Well, I need it to work better for me." Lara smiled sweetly at Meg. "I'm sure my dad won't mind if I make some adjustments."

Meg said through tight lips, "I'm sure he won't."

"It's too bad that old Edgar let Cassie lease the bakery from him. I would have done a much better job." Lara stacked mixing bowls at the end of a counter.

"Oh really?" Meg stared at her.

Lara laughed. "Of course. Cassie doesn't have it in her to run a bakery. She's much too nice. Everyone will walk right over her."

"That's not going to happen." Meg set her jaw. "Cassie has been running her cake decorating business for years and is in high demand. I have no doubt that her bakery will be even more successful."

Lara sneered at Meg. "We'll see about that. I might as well start making preparations for leasing the bakery myself. She isn't going to last long."

Between Zoe's accusations about Meg not helping and Lara's nastiness, Meg couldn't hold back any longer. "You're never getting the bakery from Cassie." Meg stuck her hands on her hips. "She's ten times the baker you'll ever be, and the only reason you got this job was because your father owns the place." She glared defiantly at Lara.

Lara's jaw dropped. "I can't believe you just said that. I'm telling my father, and he'll have your job."

Meg coolly removed her chef's jacket and let it fall to the floor. "No need for that. I quit."

Lara spun on her heels and stalked out of the room. Meg picked up the jacket and hung it on the rack, then walked toward Taylor's office with shaky legs. What had she just done? She and Zoe had agreed that she'd keep her job for a few more months. Then again, with all of the things at the Inn that hadn't gone according to plan, this was par for the course.

But what about Taylor? She'd just quit impulsively an hour before dinner service began. She hated to leave him shorthanded, but after the argument with Lara, she couldn't go back on her decision to quit.

She tapped lightly on Taylor's office door.

"Come in," he called out.

She opened the door halfway.

A smile flooded his face. "Oh good, I was worried you were Lara. I couldn't deal with her anymore." He looked past Meg. "Is the wicked witch gone for the day?"

Meg laughed at the image of Lara as a witch, then

sobered. "She's out of the kitchen, but she went to go talk to George."

"Figures." He shook his head.

Meg shuffled her feet. "I need to tell you something."

His eyes drilled into her. "What is it?"

She took a deep breath. "I told Lara that I quit."

He leaned back in his office chair and rested a hand on his chin. "Ah."

"I'm so sorry. I never meant to do it this way. You and I had talked about me staying for a few more months, but then Lara came in and was being horrible about Cassie, and—"

"And you couldn't deal with her any longer," he finished for her.

She closed her eyes briefly, then opened them, hoping he wasn't angry with her. "Yeah."

He laughed. "Well, good for you."

Her eyes widened. "You're not mad?"

"No, of course not." He sat up. "I'd give anything to tell her off, but I don't want to get fired. You have nothing to lose. Besides, I think this will be good for you. Now you'll be able to help more at the Inn, and maybe the situation with Zoe will get better."

Her cheek muscles twitched, and tears of gratitude moistened her eyes. He was being more than understanding. "Thank you."

He gave her a lopsided grin. "No problem. But do you think you could finish out the weekend?"

Meg glanced at the door. "But Lara's telling George that I quit."

"Eh." He grinned again, and stood from his chair. "Leave it to me. I'll talk to George and work things out with him. It's in his best interest to have the kitchen fully staffed until Monday, and it will give me a few days to get someone else in here." He gazed at her. "I'll never find anyone as qualified as you, though. You'll be sorely missed."

A pit filled her stomach at the thought of not seeing his smile every day. "I'm sure we'll see each other around."

He came over to her, and for a moment, she thought he was going to hug her again. Her nerves tingled as she waited for him to put his arm around her, but instead, he just patted her shoulder before leaving the office. Meg leaned against the doorframe. Her impetuous decision had opened up her life to new beginnings, but had it ended something else before it could really take hold?

14

Cassie

"Cassie, this is the best red velvet I've ever had." Denise Alvarez unwrapped the other half of her cupcake and hungrily eyed the tiered cake tray Cassie had used to display her Fourth of July treats. "Do you mind if I take one for my husband?"

"Go ahead." Cassie beamed at her. "I'm only here for another two hours, and I don't want to get stuck bringing these home with me."

Denise laughed. "I don't think I'd want to own a bakery. I'd eat all of my inventory." She licked some cream cheese frosting away from the corner of her mouth. "Are you planning on serving these cupcakes when you open?"

Cassie shrugged. "I'm not sure yet. I have so many things I want to try, but I haven't made a final list yet." A thrill shot through her. The Sea Star Bakery wouldn't officially open for another three weeks, but each day it became more real to her.

She'd made four different types of cupcakes for her

booth at the Fourth of July Community Fair to get the word out about the bakery's grand opening on July twenty-third. After agonizing over the decision for days, she'd finally selected a red velvet with cream cheese frosting, a German chocolate with a shredded coconut and chocolate topping, a classic vanilla with buttercream icing and sprinkles, and a carrot cake with the same frosting as the red velvet. They were some of her most popular choices for wedding cakes, and so far they'd been a hit with everyone in town.

"Well, I plan to be there as soon as you open." Denise threw the empty wrapper in the garbage can under the table, then selected a German chocolate cupcake for her husband, setting it on a paper napkin. "Are you planning on serving Edgar's cinnamon rolls? I hate the thought of never having one of those again."

Cassie covered the side of her mouth as though she were telling a secret and leaned over the table. "Edgar gave me the recipe before he left. Don't tell too many people, though. I don't want to be mobbed when I open."

Denise looked pointedly at the cupcakes and then at Cassie. "You're going to have a line out the door no matter what."

Cassie's chest filled with pride. "Thank you."

"I'd better get this to my husband before I eat it, but it may be missing a bite or two by the time I get to him." Denise grinned conspiratorially at Cassie. "Have fun today with the kids."

"Thanks! Oh, I almost forgot." Cassie grabbed a coupon off the stack on the table. "This will get you fifty percent off a coffee and pastry when we open."

"Thanks, Cassie." Denise accepted it. "See you when you open." She turned, and was swallowed up by the crowds milling around the vendor booths.

"Hey, Jace," Cassie said to her son, who was busy playing a game on his tablet. "You're supposed to be in charge of handing out coupons."

He looked up briefly and scanned the area in front of their table. A woman Cassie didn't recognize had approached the table and was chatting with Amanda. "I have been. I didn't see anyone here."

Cassie shook her head, but smiled. Honestly, as long as he was behaving himself, she didn't care too much about him focusing on his game. It was her weekend with the kids and she could see how sitting at their mom's booth at a fair wasn't the most exciting thing to do. The woman Amanda had been talking to left with a coupon in one hand and a cupcake in the other.

"Mom?" Amanda asked. "How much longer do we need to do this?"

Cassie assessed the number of cupcakes that were left and did some quick calculations. She'd always been good at math, a skill that came in handy when baking. "Maybe another hour? We should have given them all out by then."

Amanda sighed dramatically. "But all of my friends are here already." She looked over at a gaggle of giggling preteen girls standing off to the side of the park. "I want to go hang out with them."

Cassie stifled a grin. "You'll survive." She glanced at the girls, then back at her daughter. When she'd been Amanda's age, she'd been exactly the same, always wanting to be with her friends. "Oh, all right. You can go now."

Amanda's face lit up. "Really?"

Cassie smiled at her daughter's excitement. "Yep. But don't leave the park. When we're done here, we're going to join the Briggs family for a picnic, okay?"

"Okay." Amanda nodded vigorously. "Thanks, Mom." She ran off before Cassie could change her mind.

Cassie scanned the crowd. She knew about half of the people there, but the other half were tourists. It seemed somewhat pointless to be giving away cupcakes to people who wouldn't be in town when the bakery opened, but you never knew who was going to need a custom cake someday. She caught sight of Kyle, and her breath caught.

He was standing at the deli booth, sampling a pastrami sandwich, his favorite. But it wasn't what he was eating that had caught her eye. He was holding hands with Dana Timonds.

Cassie pressed her lips together. While she knew Kyle had been dating, she hadn't known it was Dana. Kyle and Dana had been co-workers for as long as Cassie could remember. Had he always had feelings for her?

Cassie pushed away the nasty thought as soon as it crossed her mind. He'd never given her any reason to suspect he'd been cheating on her when they were married. Now that they were divorced, he was free to date whomever he wanted. Still, it stung to see Dana smiling up at him adoringly. Dana wiped a crumb off Kyle's face, and a pang of white-hot jealousy swept over Cassie.

Cassie forced herself to look away, but not before memories of previous Willa Bay Fourth of July celebrations flooded her thoughts. The first Independence Day she and Kyle had spent together as teenagers, they'd snuck away from their families and found a quiet place down by the river to hang out. Over the years, it had become one of their favorite spots to be together, away from all the noise.

Later, when they'd had Amanda and Jace, they'd experienced the celebrations as a family, with a picnic in the park and an evening capped off by watching the fireworks display over the bay. Her stomach twisted. They'd had so many good times together, just the two of them and as a family.

But that was in the past.

She busied herself with moving the remaining cupcakes to the front of the cake stand and straightening the stack of coupons. She'd only been there for a little over an hour, and more than half of the samples were already gone. If the interest in her bakery translated into actual sales, she may very well make a success of this business.

"So, which of these do you recommend?" A deep voice asked.

Cassie looked up to see Chase Flaherty standing in front of her, flashing her a toothy grin. "They're all good, but I'm partial to the German chocolate."

He selected one of the chocolate cupcakes and slowly pulled the wrapper off one side, then took a huge bite. Cassie held her breath, waiting for his verdict. He chewed and swallowed, then gave her a thumbs-up. "These *are* delicious. I think I'm going to have to be a regular customer when you open." He winked at her, and she blushed and looked away.

"Have you found out anything new about the mural?" she asked, trying not to stare as he wiped chocolate cupcake crumbs from his lips. He'd been in the bakery once last week to take more photographs of the mural. She hadn't been around when he stopped by, so Andy had let him in.

He shook his head. "Nothing yet, but I'm not giving up. I'll let you know as soon as I do." He disposed of the napkin and grinned at her. "Maybe we could grab coffee this week to talk about it?"

Her stomach flip-flopped. Libby had been right. He

didn't have anything new to tell her about the mural, so this had to be a date. Did she want to go out with him? He seemed like the playboy type, something she normally wasn't attracted to. Then again, she and Kyle had started dating in high school, so she didn't really know if she even had a type.

"I'm not sure about this week because I have a lot going on with the bakery remodel, but maybe next week?" Cassie smiled back at him. She didn't want to say no, but the idea of saying yes to a date with Chase practically made her hyperventilate.

"Sure. Sounds good." Chase flashed her a smile that put a serious crack in her defenses.

A man walked up to the table and began asking Cassie questions about the bakery. Although he'd interrupted her conversation with Chase, she was grateful for the distraction.

"Cassie," Chase said. "I'll see you later, okay?" He winked at her again, and her stomach fluttered.

She nodded. "Have fun tonight at the celebration."

"Oh, I will." He sauntered off toward the next booth.

Chase was an attractive man, there was no arguing with that, but something was holding her back from returning his advances. The memory of Dana brushing her hand across Kyle's mouth returned, and Cassie grimaced. He'd moved on, and she needed to do the same. The next time Chase asked her to coffee – if there was a next time – she was going to accept his invitation.

"Excuse me?" The man standing in front of her said. "Can you tell me about the cupcakes?"

She shook her head slightly and smiled apologetically. "I'm so sorry, my mind was elsewhere. What can I help you with?"

She stayed at the booth until she'd given away the last

cupcake, then rolled up her display sign, the crumb-littered cake tier, and her stack of coupons. "Jace," she said. "Can you please help me bring these to the car? We'll have to make a second trip back here for the table."

After a few seconds, he looked up from his tablet. "Can we go to the playground afterward?"

She studied him, surprised that he'd voluntarily give up his tablet. "Sure. We need to get the picnic stuff out of our car and bring it to the park first, though."

"Okay." He put his tablet in his backpack and slung it over his shoulder before helping her carry everything back to her minivan, which she'd parked nearby. They folded up the table, each taking an end of it, and carried it to the van.

"Thanks, honey. I would have had a hard time managing all of that without your help." She gave him a hug, which he tolerated. She hadn't been kidding, though – at the age of nine, Jace being able to lift his end of the table and help her maneuver it back to the car saved her a lot of time and energy. Soon, he'd shoot up in height and turn into a young adult. Cassie sighed inwardly. Her baby was growing up.

She retrieved the wheeled cooler containing their food and a folded picnic blanket from the back of the van and set it on the ground. Before shutting the rear liftgate, she grabbed the leftover coupons. Might as well hand them out for the rest of the day.

She and Jace walked down to the park, located where the Willomish River entered Willa Bay. Earlier, Amanda had asked if she could go with her friend and friend's parents to the park and Cassie had agreed. Now, Cassie had a little time alone with Jace, something that didn't happen very often. Although Kyle took the kids on his weekends, Cassie didn't normally get to spend time with each kid individually. It was nice to talk to Jace about his current interests – Minecraft and sea life – without Amanda interrupting.

The big, grassy picnic area at the park was packed with people. Cassie held her hand up to her forehead as a makeshift sun visor and scanned the groups seated on colorful blankets. Libby saw her and jumped up to wave from a patchwork mosaic of blankets laid out together near the beach. Libby's sister, Meg, was already there, along with their mother, Debbie, and father, Peter.

Cassie smiled and waved back, then turned to her son. "Jace, we're over here." She pointed in the direction of Libby's family.

"Where?" He looked right at them without seeing.

"Over there. Near the beach."

He narrowed his eyes as he followed the line of her hand and pointed finger, then his expression cleared with recognition. "Oh, I see them."

They dragged the cooler over to the Briggs family and added their blanket to the others.

"Can I go play now?" Jace asked.

Cassie glanced at the playground across the lawn. Children were climbing all over the giant toy's slides and ladders like ants on a log. It wasn't right next to where they were sitting, but she could see it well enough to supervise him.

"My kids are all over there right now. William's keeping an eye on them. He's pretty responsible for an eleven-year-old," Libby reassured Cassie. "They know Jace, and he'll be fine with them."

Cassie nodded. He was old enough that she didn't need to worry too much about him going off with strangers, but with his autism and ADHD, his behavior wasn't always predictable. Still, he'd never given her any cause for concern when they were at a playground.

She touched Jace's arm to make sure she had his attention. "You can go play. Let William know you're there."

He nodded vigorously, then trotted away at a fast clip.

Cassie sat cross-legged on her blanket, and Libby slid over the ground coverings to sit next to her. "How's it going?" Libby asked. "Did people like your cupcakes?"

"I think so. They disappeared quickly, and I got a lot of questions about when the bakery will open." Cassie's stomach grumbled as she reached into the cooler for a ham and cheese sandwich she'd made that morning, and set it on a paper plate next to a bag of Doritos.

"Good." Libby grabbed a Dorito and popped it into her mouth. After crunching on it, she said, "You don't have anything to worry about. Your bakery is going to be a success."

"I hope so." Cassie bit into her sandwich. With Celia's generous offer of start-up capital and funds for renovating the bakery, Cassie hadn't had to put her house up for collateral on a small business loan, which was what had previously kept her from pursuing business ownership. Knowing that their family home was on the line would have been more stress than she could handle. However, the loan from Celia came with its own issues. Cassie didn't want to let Celia down, so the bakery had to reach profitability within a reasonable period of time.

"Do you want a sandwich?" she asked Libby.

"No, I've got a bunch in my cooler. I filled up on some fruit and cheese earlier." She stared down at the soft blanket, picking at a spot of lint that had stuck to it in the wash. "I was hoping Gabe would join me for lunch, but he hasn't shown up yet."

Cassie cocked her head to the side, her heart sinking. Her friend was hurting and there was little she could do about it. "Was he planning on coming today? Don't you usually do the Fourth as a family?"

Libby nodded. "My whole family spends the day together. It's a tradition we've done since I was a little kid." She gazed out at the bay. "Gabe used to love seeing the kids playing on the playground and making sandcastles on the beach. I don't know what's happened to him."

"You haven't talked with him yet?" Cassie asked. Libby had told her she was going to have a talk with her husband, but something must have happened to keep her from doing so.

"He's barely been home," Libby whispered. "And when he is, he locks himself in his office." She glanced at her parents and Meg, but they were busy getting supplies out for barbecuing hamburgers later. Her shoulders slumped in defeat. "I'm afraid this is the end for us."

Cassie moved closer to Libby and wrapped her arm around her friend's shoulders. Libby leaned in, furtively wiping away tears before her family could see.

"You're so lucky that at least you know things are over with Kyle," Libby said. "You can move on from that relationship and find the person you're meant to be with." Her voice cracked. "I always thought Gabe was my person."

Cassie didn't say anything, but she gently squeezed Libby's shoulder as they looked out at the waves lapping against the shoreline. She'd always thought Kyle was her person, too, and although they'd been divorced for years, she wasn't sure she was at a place yet where she *wanted* to move on from him.

15

Zoe

"When the potential clients get here, meet them in front of the Inn and linger by the gardens so they get the full effect of the property." Zoe paused in the Inn's circular driveway to make sure Tia had written down her instructions.

Tia nodded, scribbling furiously in a notebook she'd balanced in the crook of her arm. "Got it."

"Then, show them around the grounds so they can see the different areas where we can host weddings. For now, that's the area in front of the gazebo, but eventually I hope to add in some other options, including beach weddings."

"Okay." Tia looked up. "Do we have chairs available for weddings, or will clients need to rent their own?"

Zoe looked at her appraisingly. Although she'd begrudgingly allowed Shawn to hire Tia as her assistant, she'd doubted Tia would be much help. It wasn't that she wasn't qualified, it was just that Zoe preferred to oversee everything herself. Tia was asking the right questions, though, so maybe she'd be more help than Zoe expected.

"We have two hundred white chairs on order, which should be here by the end of July." Zoe looked at her watch, her stomach twisting. The first of August was only three weeks away. How could they possibly get everything done on time?

Having Tia to help was supposed to take some of the pressure off, but the time Zoe was spending to train Tia would have been better spent on working through her to-do list. Zoe had hoped that Meg quitting her job and coming to work at the Inn full time would decrease Zoe's responsibilities, but Meg hadn't been there enough to know the full breadth of everything going on with the renovations. Shawn did as much as he could, but his talents lay in managing the contractors they'd hired and performing construction work himself.

"Can we take a closer look at the gazebo?" Tia asked. "I'm sure it will be popular with potential clients, and I'd like to familiarize myself with it."

"Sure," Zoe said. "I know Shawn gave you a quick tour of the property, but let's take a more in-depth look at everything."

She spent the next two hours showing Tia around and then turned her loose to explore on her own. After Celia had spread the word that the Inn at Willa Bay would be open for weddings at the beginning of August, they'd received many phone calls inquiring about availability. Several of those had come from displaced clients of Danville Hall. Zoe had tried to take on as many of the showing appointments as she could, but Tia would need to handle some of them, including the first one later that afternoon. The person who'd made the arrangements hadn't been super enthusiastic about seeing the Inn, so

Zoe wasn't too concerned about letting Tia meet with them as her first appointment after starting the job.

Zoe was busy recording measurements for the kitchen when Meg stomped into the living room, her dark brown hair tangled and littered with tiny pieces of tree bark. Sweat beaded on her forehead, and she looked like she'd rather be at the dentist's office, undergoing a root canal.

"The next time we find a fallen tree blocking one of the walking paths, it gets left there," Meg announced as she removed her pitch-stained leather work gloves. "We'll build a step over it or something." She grabbed a glass cup from the counter and filled it from a pitcher of water, draining it in three long gulps. "I never want to move another tree trunk in my life."

Zoe grinned. "So you're giving up your dream of becoming a logger?"

Meg glared at her. "Haha. Very funny." She sighed. "Shawn made rolling away the cut pieces look so easy, but it was ten times harder than lifting weights at the gym." Meg eyed her with suspicion. "Hey, how come you don't have to help with clearing the trails?"

As if she hadn't spent countless hours over the last two months pulling weeds, tearing out blackberry vines, and, yes, clearing the trails. Zoe put down her pen and stared at Meg. She tried to keep her voice cool as she answered. "I've put in plenty of time on the trails. Today, I had to finish up the plans for the kitchen. If we want to host weddings here in a few weeks, we've got to get this place put back together."

"I could help you inside," Meg said. "I've spent half my life in kitchens, remember?"

"I know, but there are only a few things left to decide on for the remodel." Zoe gestured to her paper. "I'm actually almost done."

Meg refilled her water glass, taking small sips this time. "What's on the agenda for this afternoon? Am I working on the trails again?" Now that she'd rehydrated and cooled off, her tone lightened. "I suppose this is what I deserved after talking about how much I missed going to the gym. I had to cancel my membership after we bought the Inn because I didn't have time to go there."

Zoe consulted her planner, which she'd crowded with a hodgepodge of colorful inked appointment reminders and project deadlines. "I have a meeting later today with the kitchen contractor to finalize everything, and you're probably right – it would be good to have you join me for that meeting. I don't want to miss anything crucial."

"Anything that doesn't involve work gloves is fine with me." Meg cast a withering glare at the gloves she'd set on a plastic side table. "What's Tia up to today? I saw her wandering around outside earlier."

Zoe took a deep breath. "She's taking our first potential client on a tour."

Meg's eyebrows rose. "Do you think she's okay on her own?"

Every bone in Zoe's body screamed *NO* and the muscles in her face tensed in response, but she pasted on what she hoped would pass for a confident smile. "Uh-huh. She'll do fine. She's experienced in event planning, so I'm not worried."

"Right ..." Meg shook her head. "I can always tell when you're lying. Your cheek is twitching like a bunny's nose right now."

Zoe ran her fingers over the telltale sign that had been a giveaway since she was a kid. She'd never be a professional poker player, but it kept her honest. "Okay. So I'm a little concerned. But Shawn insisted that I give up a little control, and this appointment doesn't seem too important. At this point, discussing the kitchen remodel with our contractor is a higher priority for my time."

"If you say so." Meg set her cup on the table. "Now, what are we going to go over with the kitchen contractor? I'm excited to see how things are coming along."

Hours later, Tia came into the living room, where Zoe was sitting on the couch with her iPad, flipping between two different images of flooring as she attempted to make her umpteenth decision of the day.

"I've got good news," Tia sang out.

Zoe looked up sharply. "Did they like the property?"

"No," Tia said, then broke out into a 100-watt smile. "They loved it."

Zoe smiled. "That's great. Did they want to sign a contract?"

Tia nodded. "They're coming in tomorrow to sign it. They're one of the displaced clients of Danville Hall and desperately need to find a venue for their August eighth wedding. The bride-to-be is going to bring her mom with her to see the Inn's grounds. She said there aren't many places in the area where you can have a beach wedding, so that was a huge draw."

Zoe's eyes bugged out. "A beach wedding? Did you promise them they could get married on the beach?"

"Yeah, why?" Tia shuffled her feet. "Isn't that okay?"

"For an August eighth wedding? I told you we wouldn't have the beach ready for ceremonies for a couple of months." Zoe dropped the tablet to her lap and stared up at the ceiling, mentally calculating what they'd need to do to make a beach wedding possible. Repairing the stairs down to the beach had been one of the first things Shawn had done when he'd moved to Willa Bay, but they hadn't had time yet to add the finishing touches to the beach access to make it shine, nor clear the driftwood on the beach to accommodate wedding guests.

"Oh. I'm so sorry. I must have misunderstood." Tia bit her lip. "I'll have to tell them tomorrow that we'll need to do a wedding by the gazebo. They were quite taken with it as well, so it'll probably be fine. But they were really excited about the idea of a beach wedding."

Zoe sighed. In her role as a wedding coordinator while she'd been employed at the Willa Bay Lodge, she'd never been charged with making the final decisions on any event. Her boss, Joan, had made it look so easy to accommodate unusual client requests. Now that Zoe was an owner and manager of the Inn at Willa Bay, and working the equivalent of the event manager job she'd hoped to be promoted to at the Lodge, Zoe would be tasked with making those decisions. Managing employees and being ultimately responsible for events was just as much of an adjustment for her as it was for Tia starting this new job.

"Okay. Let me think about this for a while." Zoe got up from the couch and set her iPad on a side table. "I'm going to take a walk and then we can discuss this further."

Tia nodded. "I'm really sorry, Zoe. I didn't mean to mess anything up."

Zoe gave her a small smile. "I'm sure it'll be fine." Her breath was ragged now, and the walls were closing in on her. If she didn't get some fresh air soon, she was worried she might have a panic attack. She'd always had anxiety, but had never come close to a full-fledged panic attack until recently. One time in college, a friend of hers had been hit with one, and it had been terrifying to watch. Zoe wanted to do anything she could to manage her anxiety before it happened to her too.

She hurried out the door and into the front yard, then

jogged to the beach, not paying attention to anyone along the way. The beach was her happy place, somewhere she could turn whenever things got difficult. It wasn't a magic cure, but today the sound of the waves crashing on the shore almost instantly dulled the sharp edge of her stress.

On impulse, she took her phone out of the pocket of her lightweight, zip-up jacket and dialed her brother.

"Luke?" she asked when it connected.

"Hey sis."

"Is this a good time to talk?" She bit her lip, realizing just how much she'd needed to talk to him.

"Of course. Is everything okay?" he asked, his voice tinged with concern.

She took a deep breath of the sea air. "Yeah. Just a little stressed."

"Is there anything I can do to help?"

"I don't know." Zoe drew a circle in the sand with the toe of her shoe. "It's just that I didn't think this would be so hard." She glanced up at the Inn and her anxiety levels heightened. She quickly averted her gaze and faced the water, letting the rhythm of the waves bring her heart rate back down.

"You didn't think renovating a rundown resort property would be stressful?" Luke asked dryly.

"Maybe not this bad?" She sighed. "I know. I was naive to think it wouldn't be too bad."

"Is everything working out?" His words were softer now.

"I think so. Or it will be soon." She peeked up at the Inn, frowning at the deteriorating shingles on the roof. "Was it this challenging for you when you started the food truck?" Luke owned a barbecue food truck in Candle Beach, which, from her point of view, had been an immediate success.

He laughed. "It wasn't easy. I had to hunt down the truck, make a ton of repairs, then figure out how to run a food truck business. There were so many moving pieces that I often thought I'd never get the restaurant off of the ground." A dreamy quality came over his voice, and she imagined him staring at his food truck. "But now here I am, a business owner. I love what I do, and I wouldn't trade it for the world. I can't say I felt the same way as a software developer. My job at the tech company wasn't nearly as satisfying as being my own boss and having a direct impact on a business."

"So, you think things will get better for me?" She paced in circles, letting the small exertion remove some of her excess energy.

"I'm sure they will. I have faith in you. No matter what, you'll find a way to make your dream happen." He sighed. "I guess what I'm saying is that this part of the process is short-term, and it will all be worth it when you're looking at what you've earned through your own hard work."

"Thanks, Luke." She let her body stop moving and relaxed her tensed muscles.

"Did that help at all? I'm sure everyone's experience is different, but I personally am grateful every day that I took the plunge."

"Yeah. I feel a little better about everything now." A gust of wind blew her hair sideways, and she tucked the errant strands back behind her ears. "I'd better get back and face the music, but I appreciate your words of wisdom."

"No problem. I'm glad to help," he said. "Oh, Pops and I were thinking about coming out to see you in about two weeks. Does that work for you?"

A rush of longing came over her. It had only been a few months since she'd visited Candle Beach and seen her brother and grandfather, but the thought of seeing their faces again brought tears of joy to her eyes. They'd always been so supportive, and right now she could use all the support she could get.

"I'd be thrilled if you both came to visit. Bring Charlotte, too, if you want. I'd love to see her again. The rooms at the Inn won't be open yet, but Pops can take the bedroom in my cottage if he wants to stay overnight. I'm sure we can find somewhere for the two of you to sleep too."

"Don't even worry about it," Luke said. "I'll book us some rooms in town. I wanted to check with you first before I made reservations or invited Charlotte and Pops, but I'll take care of that tonight. And Zoe?"

"Yeah?"

"I'm looking forward to seeing you and getting a first-hand look at everything you've done with the Inn."

"Well, Shawn and Meg helped a little." She laughed. "Okay, more than a little. But I'm looking forward to seeing you, too, and giving you an update on our progress here."

She hoped he'd like what he saw on his visit. He had faith in her abilities to renovate the old property, and had been the one to invest in her, Shawn, and Meg so they could purchase a half-interest in the resort from Celia. But she still wanted him to feel like his money had been well-spent.

She put her phone away and surveyed the area near the stairs to the beach, assessing it as though she were a wedding guest. They'd need to cut away some of the bigger pieces of driftwood and sweep the seaweed and kelp off the sand before a ceremony, but with the peaceful sound of the waves lapping at the shore and the soft breezes rustling the seagrass, it would be an enchanting venue. They were a beach resort, so they might as well start off right by offering weddings on the sand, even if it meant more work before they opened.

She returned to the Inn where Tia was sitting on the porch, nervously tapping her pen against her notebook. She popped up when Zoe climbed the stairs to the front door and followed her inside.

"Are you okay?" she asked. "You left so suddenly. I was worried, but I didn't want to chase after you if you wanted some time to yourself."

Zoe smiled, and for the first time in a while, could answer that question honestly. "I'm okay." She led Tia into the living room where she'd left her iPad. "We'll figure out a way to make it work." Zoe gestured for Tia to sit next to her on the couch. "Let's talk about the rest of the client's details so we're on the same page when they return to sign their contract."

Tia perched on the couch, turning her knees to face Zoe. She recited the information she'd scribbled in her notebook, and Zoe used the iPad to enter it into their brand-new event management system. Tia had been thorough in recording all of the client's personal information, along with their requests and her suggestions. Zoe hated to admit it, but with the exception of her mistake in promising a beach wedding, hiring Tia hadn't been such a bad idea.

When they finished, Tia went home for the day and Zoe pulled out her to-do list, adding the tasks necessary to host a beach wedding. The list was getting longer instead of shorter, but she took heart in Luke's conviction that everything would work out.

The door to the living room opened, and Celia entered with her walker, a huge smile lighting up her face. "How much do you love me?" she teased.

Her good humor was contagious, and Zoe grinned back at her. "A lot," Zoe answered. They had never truly bonded in the ten years Zoe rented the cottage from Celia, but since Celia's accident last April and seeing how much her friends cared for her, she had let her guard down and become like a bonus grandmother – one Zoe felt lucky enough to get to see every day. "But why do I love you today?"

"Because I found you a roofer." Celia's blue eyes sparkled in her wizened face. "I called in a few favors, and Blue Bay Roofing is going to start on Monday."

Zoe's pulse quickened, and she couldn't do anything but gape at Celia for several seconds. "Blue Bay is one of the most highly rated roofers around," Zoe said. "How did you get them to come out here, especially on short notice?"

Celia shrugged. "I told you. I know people." She wiggled her eyebrows and laughed. "Seriously, though, they were supposed to work on the roof of Danville Hall. I found out about the gap in their schedule and nabbed them immediately for the Inn."

Zoe sprang from the couch and ran over to Celia, being careful not to knock the elderly woman over as she wrapped her arms around her. "Thank you. I can't even tell you how much I appreciate this." She stepped back and looked at Celia. "Thank you so much."

Celia smiled, pink cheeks creasing. "No problem. I want to see this Inn succeed just as much as you do." A far-off expression came over her face, as though she were remembering good times at the Inn. "But now, this old woman needs a nap." She swiveled her walker around. "I'll see you for dinner, right?"

"Right." Zoe chuckled. You never knew what to expect with Celia.

After Celia left, Zoe went out to the back porch, hooking her arm around one of the posts she and Cassie had painted a few weeks earlier. The worries that weighed her down had lifted, and she could see the light at the end of the tunnel. Luke had been right. Everything was going to be okay.

16

Kyle

"These are the cans of pie filling that time forgot." With both hands, Kyle held up a dust-covered commercial-sized can of cherry pie filling to show Cassie. He rubbed the side of the can clean to read the date printed on it. "It's frightening that they don't expire for another year."

Cassie wrinkled her nose. "That *is* frightening." She took the giant can from him and stacked it in the corner of the small storeroom. "I bet Edgar had them here as a back-up plan, because as far as I know, he only used freshly made fillings for his pastries."

Kyle eyed the rack they were emptying, which still contained an entire row of various fruit pie fillings. "He must have been expecting quite a baking emergency."

Cassie giggled, filling Kyle's heart with joy. He'd known her since they were teenagers, and hearing her laugh always made him happy. When he'd called to ask if it was okay for the kids to visit his parents for the weekend, she'd mentioned plans to clean out the storeroom at the bakery. He'd offered to help her with the project since they'd both be kid-free, something that didn't happen very often.

"I'm about ready for a break. What do you think?" she asked.

He dusted his hands off on his blue jeans. "I could do with a cup of coffee and a donut." He followed her out of the tiny storeroom and down the short hallway to the front of the bakery.

As she poured them each a cup of drip coffee from an old filter-style coffee pot on the counter, Kyle took the opportunity to look around. It was the first time he'd been in there since Cassie took over, and he liked the changes she'd made. Her contractors had moved the counter slightly to create a better space for the flow of customers on busy days, and they'd somehow managed to form a bigger indoor eating area with more tables than had been there previously.

Cassie came out from behind the counter with a mug of steaming coffee in each hand. She set them on a table for two, then grabbed a box of donuts she'd bought from a shop down the street.

"I feel odd serving you someone else's donuts in my bakery, but we're not exactly up and running yet." She made a face at the line of storage containers on the counter.

"I'm not complaining." Kyle grinned as he selected a cinnamon-sugar twist from the pink cardboard box. "These have always been my favorite." He bit into the donut, letting the sugar melt on his tongue.

"I know," Cassie said softly. "I was glad they still had some left when I bought them this morning."

She'd remembered what he liked. He'd been about to

take another bite, but halted with the donut midway to his mouth. "Thanks for thinking of me."

She shrugged. "I was buying them anyway. I figured I might as well get something you liked since you were so kind to help me today."

He nodded and finished off the cinnamon twist in a few bites. Cassie nibbled on her raspberry-filled donut, leaving a trace of red jelly on her lips.

"You've got a little something on your mouth," he said, oddly fascinated by the red smudge.

Her tongue slid out, and she daintily licked her lips. His chest constricted. Even after all these years, he couldn't deny an attraction to her. *She's your ex-wife, Kyle. Get a grip on yourself.*

Maybe this had been a mistake. He took a swig of coffee, then cleared his throat and stood, searching for a distraction. The mural on the wall caught his eye and he walked over to it.

"So, this is the famous mural." He let his eyes slide over the painting, noting the little vignettes of life that the artist had tucked into different areas of the landscape. The rocks and trees looked familiar, but he couldn't place them. "Have you found out anything about who painted it?"

Cassie shook her head. "Not yet." She joined him in front of the mural and sighed. "It's so beautiful. Every time I see it, I can't help but remember waking up in Monterey to that beautiful view."

As if in a trance, he took another look at the entirety of the mural – the twisted trees, the rolling dunes, and the waves beating against the rocky jetties. This was definitely the central California coast. How had he missed that?

Maybe you didn't want to see it, chided a little voice inside his head. He stared at the wall. Their honeymoon on the Monterey Peninsula had been everything he could have asked for – romantic, exciting, and full of discoveries about his new wife. An image popped into his mind of Cassie standing on a stone ledge at the edge of the beach, the water ricocheting off the rock and misting her with the spray. She'd squealed and spun around, directly into his arms. They'd stood there, locked in a lover's embrace, taking in together the raw, natural beauty of the coast.

"Kyle?" Cassie asked, interrupting the movie playing in his mind.

He blinked his eyes and focused on the woman who was now his ex-wife. "Yeah. Sorry. I was lost in thought. Did you say something?"

"I was just wondering if you were ready to get back to work." Her eyes searched his face, and she sighed. "I love this mural, but sometimes I wonder if it would've been better to have the construction crew remove the panels."

"Why?" He turned away from the mural to keep from having any more thoughts about their honeymoon. "It's beautiful."

She shrugged. "Every time I see it, it brings back so many old memories." Her eyes were bright, and he could tell she was trying to keep from looking at the mural too.

He locked eyes with her. "Is that so bad?"

"I don't know," she whispered. "Sometimes it's a little too much." She uttered a small laugh and flashed him a smile. "Wow, that got deep really fast. I'm going to head back to the storeroom." She pivoted quickly and disappeared from sight.

Kyle allowed himself a last peek at the painting, and was hit with a wave of longing for how things used to be between him and Cassie. He tore his gaze away from it. Both of them had moved on. He was dating an amazing woman, and Cassie was taking some much-deserved time to figure out what she wanted from life. What they'd had together in the beginning had been special, but some things just weren't meant to be.

He took a deep breath and joined her in the storeroom, both of them keeping the conversation purposefully light. After they'd finished wiping down the shelves and re-organizing the cans, they stood awkwardly together near the back door to the bakery.

"Well, thank you for all of your help." Cassie stepped forward and gave him a hug. Her familiar, lightly scented floral perfume surrounded him, and the softness of her touch made it difficult to breathe. He froze in place, unable to reciprocate the embrace. Her cheeks turned pink, and she quickly retreated. "I'm sorry. That was weird, wasn't it?"

He forced a small smile, his heart still beating faster than normal. "A little."

Her face fell. "I'm sorry. I didn't mean to make things weird between us."

"No worries. I was just caught off guard. I'll see you later, okay?" He turned and exited the building before she could say anything else. Once outside, with Cassie safely on the other side of the door, he took several deep breaths. Had she noticed how much he'd enjoyed having her close?

They'd worked so hard to reach an amicable relationship – for the kids' sake, if not each other's. These feelings he had for Cassie were nothing but memories, so for everyone's benefit, he needed to shake them – ASAP.

∾

"Kyle. Are you listening to anything I've been saying?" Dana peered at him from the other side of their table at Roger's Grill.

After ordering their entrees, Dana had launched into a description of the tourist town she'd visited the weekend before on a girls' getaway trip. He'd tried to keep his attention on her, but after hearing about three wineries that sounded remarkably similar, he'd found his thoughts drifting. During the few hours he'd spent in the bakery with Cassie earlier that day, he'd felt more alive than he had in a long time. The feelings and memories evoked by the mural had taken hold in his brain and wouldn't let go.

"I am. You were telling me about the wineries." He sipped the ruby-red Merlot he'd ordered and made a face. "I hope their wine was better than this."

Dana laughed. "What did you expect from the house wine?"

He shrugged. "Maybe too much." Dana had been wanting to go to Roger's and he'd thought the romantic restaurant would take his mind off Cassie, so he'd made reservations when he got home from the bakery. He looked around. It had tablecloths, candlelight, and prices on the menu that were more than he usually spent on a month's worth of groceries.

Dana had been thrilled when he'd told her about the dinner reservation. She was stunning in a little black dress that showed off her svelte figure. A thick silver necklace and matching earrings accented the cut of the dress, and her cheeks were flushed prettily from the glass of Chablis she'd already consumed. He couldn't have asked for a more beautiful date or perfect setting, so why did he feel like he'd rather be somewhere else?

The waiter approached their table holding their

Caesar salads and placed the plates in front of them on the linen tablecloth.

"Looks good." Kyle shoveled a large forkful of dressing-coated lettuce into his mouth. If he was eating, Dana couldn't expect him to talk – and right now, he didn't think he was in the right headspace to carry on a conversation with her. With any luck, he was out of sorts because of hunger, and the delicious food would bring him back to his senses.

She stared at him and poked her fork into her salad, taking a much smaller bite than he had. The waiter came by to check on them, and she requested another drink, which he brought to her a few minutes later. The busboy cleared the plates as soon as they were done with their salads, then, as if by magic, the waiter appeared with their entrées.

Dana drained the last drop of wine from her glass and signaled the waiter to bring another. Kyle raised his eyebrows. In all the years he'd known her, she'd never been a big drinker. "Is everything okay?" His knife and fork hovered over his steak as he waited for her answer.

"Uh-huh." She sawed at her steak with the serrated knife and quickly put a bite in her mouth.

He set his utensils down. "Dana, what's wrong? Is it something I did?"

She finished chewing and washed it down with a gulp of wine. Her eyes wavered as she tried to meet his gaze. "You spent the day with Cassie today, right?"

"Yeah, why?" He'd told her earlier that he had helped Cassie at the bakery, but hadn't gone into too much detail.

"Were your kids there?"

"No, they were with my parents." He scanned her face. "Does it upset you that Cassie and I still talk?"

She sighed. "Talk, no. The fact that you're obviously

still in love with your ex-wife, yes. That does bother me." She took another long drink and set the glass on the table with a muffled thud before staring directly at him.

Her words hit him with the force of a freight train. "I'm not still in love with Cassie."

She looked down at her food and pressed her lips together. "Are you sure about that?"

He sat back in his chair, his heart beating wildly. Was she right? Memories of happy times with his ex-wife flooded over him, followed closely by images of the not-so-happy times. Even if a spark remained between the two of them, they'd already determined they weren't compatible.

"I'm sure," he said. "There's nothing between Cassie and me, other than the kids."

"If that was true, you wouldn't jump at the chance to spend time with her." Dana removed the cloth napkin from her lap and wiped the corner of her mouth. "I invited you to go with me to Seattle this morning, but, instead, you spent the day with her."

"I'd already promised her that I'd help with the bakery." Even to him, his statement sounded lame. He should have been excited at the prospect of a day trip with his girlfriend, but he'd chosen to spend the time with his ex-wife.

"I get that, and I know your kids will always come first, but I didn't expect to compete for your time with your ex-wife too." She sighed and folded her napkin into fourths before setting it on the table. "Look, I really like you, but I don't think this is going to work out."

He ran his fingers through his hair. "I can tell her that I can't spend time with her anymore."

She shook her head sadly. "But that's not what you want."

Was she right? After all this time, was he not over Cassie? A mixture of fear and excitement reverberated throughout his body, and he lifted his eyes to meet hers. "I didn't mean to hurt you."

She gave him a small smile. "You didn't. I think part of me always knew that you weren't actually available."

"Is this going to be awkward at work?" he asked. "I'd hate for this to affect our working relationship."

She took a deep breath. "I've received a job offer for a principal position from a firm in Seattle. It'll be a promotion and a nice bump in salary."

"And you won't have to worry about seeing me every day." He sighed and rested his forearms on the table. "I'm really sorry."

She reached across the table and covered his hand in hers. "Don't be. I hope you and Cassie get your second chance."

"Thank you." He hooked his thumb over her fingers and squeezed them gently before withdrawing his hand. "I wish you all the best in your new job."

"Thank you." She stood from the table, gave him a peck on the cheek, and whispered, "Good luck." Then she strode away without looking back.

17

Cassie

Cassie's phone buzzed just as she slid the last roll of register tape onto the shelf under the bakery's service counter.

Chase had texted her. *Come find me as soon as you have a chance,* it read. *I have good news about the mural!*

She glanced over at the painting. Was she finally going to solve the mystery of the artist? There was nothing urgent for her to do at the bakery, so she locked the front door and walked quickly down Main Street to the art gallery.

When she entered, Chase was in the middle of helping a customer, so she occupied herself with checking out some of the paintings by a local artist. One in particular caught her eye: a young boy wading through a tidepool to examine a sea star suctioned onto the side of a boulder stuck in the sand. It reminded her so much of Jace that she immediately wanted to buy it – until she saw the price tag. Sadly, she turned away, almost running into

Chase, who'd snuck up on her while she'd been admiring the artwork.

"Do you like it?" Chase gestured to the painting.

She nodded. "Very much, but it's a little out of my price range." More like *way* out of her price range.

He smiled. "Let me show you something." He led her over to a rack of prints and dug through it, pulling out a smaller version of the painting she'd admired. "How about this?"

She turned it over to view the price, then beamed. "It's perfect. I'll take it."

He rang up the print, then wrapped it in tissue paper before placing it in a paper bag with handles made of a thick twine. "Now, are you ready for my news?" He held out the bag to her.

"I am. What have you found out?" She accepted the bag and peered at him.

"Come with me." He took her into the back room and gestured for her to sit down at a long table that, judging by the scraps of packing materials on it, was used for wrapping art prior to shipment.

Every second he held off on telling her about what he'd found only increased her curiosity. "So, who painted it?"

"Ah," he said. "That's a fascinating story." He sat down at the table and reached for an iPad, tapping away at it. "One of my colleagues who saw the photos of the mural thought he recognized the style. Turns out, he was right." He turned the iPad toward her, revealing images of several paintings similar to the one on the wall of her bakery.

She leaned closer to get a better look. "Wow. Those are stunning." She looked up into his sparkling blue eyes. "They're all of Monterey and Big Sur. Does the artist live there?"

He shook his head. "No. She was born in that area but moved to Willa Bay back in the 1920s. She lived around here until her death in 1997."

"Oh." Some of Cassie's happiness deflated. It may have been silly, but she'd felt a connection to the artist because of their shared love of the Central California coast. "So, who was she?"

"Her name was Sofia Valencia Parker." He wiggled his eyebrows at her. "Want to know more?"

"I'd love to." Cassie sighed. "I really wish I could have met her. Every time I see the mural, it seems to speak to me. I would've loved to meet the creator to find out why she painted it on the bakery wall and what it meant to her. It has almost a sad quality to it."

"Well, there's not much I can do about meeting the artist, but I can introduce you to her granddaughter. She's offered to meet with us and answer as many of your questions as she can."

She stared at him. "That would be amazing. Does she live around here?"

He gave her a wide smile. "She does. If you'd like, I can see if she can meet with us this afternoon."

Cassie nodded vigorously. "Yes. Please call her."

He took his phone out of his pants pocket and dialed a number he'd recorded on his iPad. It rang a few times, then a woman's voice rang out over the speaker.

"Hello? This is Dr. Parker. How may I help you?"

"Hi, Sofia. This is Chase Flaherty, from the art gallery in town. I'm with Cassie, the owner of the bakery where we found your grandmother's mural. We were wondering if we could meet with you to discuss it and your grandmother. Maybe today?"

The woman hesitated. "Let's see. I have appointments

all morning, but I could meet you at my office at one thirty, if that works for you."

Chase lifted an eyebrow at Cassie. She nodded, and he said, "One thirty is great. See you then."

"Dr. Parker ..." Cassie wracked her brain trying to remember where she'd heard that name. "Her name sounds so familiar."

"She's a family physician here in town," Chase said. "I think she's only lived here for a year or two, though."

Loud voices carried into the back room, and Chase peeked into the retail area. He turned back to Cassie. "I think a tour bus just dropped people off at the corner. I'd better get back to help my assistant, but I'll pick you up from the bakery at one fifteen, if that's okay."

She nodded. "I'll see you then." She followed him out into the front and wove her way through the shoppers to reach the door. Once free of the crowd, she paused on the sidewalk. Dealing with the tourist crowds was going to take some getting used to once she opened the bakery. In her previous job at the Willa Bay Lodge, she'd worked behind the scenes. Now, as a bakery owner, unless she wanted to be baking all day, she was often going to be at the register helping customers directly.

Cassie went home for lunch, then returned to the bakery to work on her supply orders until Chase was scheduled to arrive. It should have been a simple task, but her attention kept straying to the mural. She sighed, closed the lid on her laptop, then rose from her chair and walked over to the painted landscape.

She lightly touched the painting and imagined the artist's brush moving over that spot. Why had Sofia Valencia Parker chosen this location for such a massive painting? The huge undertaking must have taken months, if not years. Cassie stepped back. In another hour, she'd have her answer.

When Chase showed up at the bakery door, Cassie was ready to go. They walked about eight blocks to an area on the outskirts of the downtown area where historic houses had been converted into businesses. Dr. Sofia Parker's office took up a forest green Victorian with brick-red trim. Six steps led up to a door with a plaque on it bearing the doctor's name. Cassie was unfamiliar with this house and the doctor, but her family dentist was just down the block.

Chase opened the door for them, and they stepped into a small hallway with an ornate patterned rug leading into an open living room that served as a waiting area. A woman wearing a long white coat stood with her back to them, reading a patient file.

She turned when she heard them enter and smiled at them. "You must be Chase and Cassie."

Cassie nodded and held out her hand. "Cassie Thorsen. Nice to meet you."

"Sofia Parker. It's nice to meet you." She shook hands with both Cassie and Chase, who also introduced himself to her. "Come with me." She led them out of the room and down the hallway, turning a corner before reaching a smaller room with a desk and three chairs. She sat down behind her desk and motioned for them to take a seat. "Ever since you called, I've been looking forward to meeting you and finding out about this mural you've uncovered."

"Yes. We've been looking forward to seeing you too," Chase said smoothly. "Cassie's been quite anxious to find out more about your grandmother." He flashed Cassie a brilliant smile.

Cassie sat in the offered chair and smiled at Sofia. "I

appreciate you taking the time to meet with us. You must be very busy here."

Sofia shrugged. "I had a gap in my schedule, and this is important." She leaned forward, across the desk. "While I was growing up, I heard stories about the mural my grandmother had painted, but was told that when my grandparents sold the building, the mural was destroyed."

Laughter bubbled out of Cassie's throat as she pictured the massive mural. "Oh no, it's very much there, taking up an entire wall in my bakery. I'd planned to put in an eating area along that wall, but when we found the artwork, I had to change some things up."

"Really?" Sofia's eyes sparkled. "An entire wall? I'd love to see it sometime."

"Anytime." Cassie scooted to the front of her chair. "Can you tell me about your grandmother? Were you close to her?"

"Well, I'm named after her. You can't get much closer than that." Sofia laughed. "Seriously, though, Abuela Sofia died when I was fourteen, so I grew up listening to her stories about her home in California and her marriage to my grandfather. She had quite an interesting life."

Chase nodded. "After I talked to you the first time, I did a little research on her. It seems she only painted scenes from California. Why is that?"

A far-off look came into Sofia's eyes. "It's really quite romantic. Abuela grew up on a ranch near the Monterey Peninsula that had been in her family for generations. When she was a teenager, she fell madly in love with Joseph, a young man she'd met in town, and eventually they married." She uttered a long sigh. "Unfortunately, Grandpa Joe had a streak of wanderlust in him, and he'd heard about the prosperity in Seattle. He wanted to head north, but Abuela wouldn't agree to it. She loved where they lived and couldn't imagine living anywhere else. They quarreled frequently until finally, he left on his new adventure, leaving Abuela at home with her family."

Cassie held her breath. Was this why there was such passion in the artist's rendition of the coast?

"So what happened? Did they get divorced? How did she end up in Willa Bay?" Chase asked, clearly just as enraptured as Cassie by Sofia's story.

Sofia grinned. "After two years apart, Abuela realized that California wasn't home anymore. Wherever Grandpa Joe lived was where she needed to be. She packed up as many belongings as she could fit into a suitcase and came up here. In the years they'd been separated, he had done well for himself. He'd been in the right place at the right time, eventually earned enough money to buy an existing building in the newly built resort town of Willa Bay, and opened a mercantile offering groceries and dry goods. When he and Abuela reunited, they moved into the small apartment above the store."

"Was that the bakery?" Cassie asked. The building housing the bakery must have seen so many different incarnations over the years.

Sofia shook her head. "No. Soon after Abuela arrived in Willa Bay, there was a terrible fire that ripped through that part of town. It burned several businesses, including the store and their apartment. Everything Abuela had brought with her from home was lost in the fire – photos of her family, old letters, everything. The fire started at night, and they barely escaped with their lives."

"Oh no." Cassie swallowed a lump in her throat, not even wanting to think about what that would be like. How painful it must have been for Sofia Valencia to lose all of her belongings, especially being so far away from everything she'd ever known. "So, they rebuilt?"

"They did," Sofia said. "Abuela was so homesick that Grandpa Joe had the building rebuilt in the Spanish Revival architectural style that had become popular in Abuela's hometown and other communities along the California coast. He figured it would give Abuela a taste of home, but be appropriate for attracting tourists in Willa Bay. It took several years to construct, and townspeople thought he was crazy, but he wanted to do it for the woman he loved."

Cassie took a deep breath. "Wow."

"I know." Sofia laughed. "If only I could find a man like that. Grandpa realized he shouldn't have left Abuela behind, and he tried to make it up to her the best way he knew how." She smiled sadly. "They were married for over fifty years, but he passed away before I was born. From all the stories about him that Abuela told me, I would have loved to have known him."

"When did she paint the mural?" Cassie asked.

"As soon as the walls were up in the new construction," Sofia said. "From what she said, she painted it in what used to be the section of the store where they sold fabric, home furnishings, and other dry goods." She shook her head from side to side. "I never thought I'd ever see it." She peered at Cassie. "Is it as beautiful as I've heard?"

Happiness spread through Cassie as she pictured the mural. "It's gorgeous. Your grandmother was a wonderful artist."

"I know." Sofia pointed to the wall behind them, and both Cassie and Chase turned to face it. "I have a few of her paintings here and some more at home. When I look at them, it's like Abuela is right here with me, telling me about her life back in California."

The art on the wall was in the same style as the mural,

depicting a sunny day on the coast. Sofia Valencia had captured the way the sun bounced off the rocks and water, filling the sky with a warm light.

Chase admired the painting. "She was very talented. If I ever see any of her work for sale, I'll be sure to purchase it."

"Abuela only sold a few pieces, so they'll be difficult to find," Sofia said. "She was a perfectionist and often would spend months on one painting. But the results were worth it."

Chase nodded. "I agree."

They all looked at the painting for another minute, then Sofia cleared her throat. "I have a patient coming in soon, but I'd love to see the mural sometime."

Cassie tore her eyes away from the coastal scene. "Come by the bakery any time. Would you mind if I put a short description of your grandmother and her story on the wall next to it? I'll run it by you first, of course."

Sofia's eyes were bright as she said, "I think Abuela would have liked that. Thank you." She glanced at the door. "I'd better get going, but thank you both so much for telling me about the mural. I'm excited to see it soon." She sighed. "It's like finding a little piece of my grandmother that I didn't know existed."

They all stood from their chairs, and she showed them to the front door.

"Thank you again for meeting with us." Cassie instinctively gave Sofia a brief hug, which the other woman returned. "I've been wondering about this mural for weeks, and it's so good to finally know more about the artist."

"No, thank *you* for giving me this gift." Sofia shook Chase's hand. "I'll be in touch." She smiled at them both, then walked into the waiting room.

Cassie and Chase left the doctor's office, pausing outside on the sidewalk.

"That was something," he said, smiling at her. "Can I interest you in a cup of coffee? I have some time before I need to be back at the gallery."

She checked her watch. It was later than she'd thought. "I'd better get home before the kids do."

"Oh." His face fell. "Well, if coffee doesn't work, would you like to have dinner with me sometime? Maybe on a weekend that the kids are with your ex?"

She studied his face. His attention was flattering, but was she ready to start dating again? Did she even want to? Her heart beat faster.

Sofia Valencia had given up everything she'd ever known to take a chance on moving north to be with her husband. She and Joseph had gone through their own issues, but things had eventually worked out between them. According to Sofia Parker, her grandparents had been wildly happy after getting back together. Was there hope that Cassie and Kyle could do the same?

Even if there wasn't, Cassie didn't want to lead Chase on.

She smiled at him apologetically. "I'm sorry, but I don't think so. It's not a good time for me to be dating right now. Everything in my life is a little topsy-turvy."

He nodded. "I understand. If you ever change your mind, let me know." He flashed her a wide grin that should have made her reconsider, but she knew in her heart that she'd made the right decision. "I'll see you later." He touched her arm lightly, then walked away, whistling under his breath.

When Cassie was alone, she was filled with uncertainty. Should she tell Kyle how she felt about him? Her ex-husband was dating someone else. Would it be better to just let the matter go and hope the feelings resolved?

They'd been divorced for a couple of years already – *would* the feelings ever go away? She took the long way home, circling the park, hoping the exercise would bring her clarity. Unfortunately, by the time she unlocked the front door of her house, she wasn't any closer to making a decision.

18

Libby

Libby scrubbed at the frying pan, scraping off the remnants of the cheesy scrambled eggs she'd made everyone for breakfast. The soap bubbles floated high in the air, refracting the sunlight into tiny rainbows, cheering her momentarily. She'd arranged for her parents to take the kids overnight in hopes of finally talking to Gabe alone. Not knowing what was going on with him was eating away at her. She'd snapped at her kids more than usual that week, and it wasn't fair to them. Something had to give.

He was late getting home, which shouldn't have surprised her because it was becoming the norm. He needed to show up soon, though, before she chickened out of confronting him about his behavior. She rinsed the pan off and stuck it in the dish drainer, then moved on to the other items in the sink. As her stack of dirty dishes dwindled, her resolve strengthened. It didn't matter when her husband came home, they were going to settle this tonight.

The front door opened and Gabe's footsteps sounded on the floor of the entry hall. Libby stuck the last plate into the dishwasher and punched the buttons to run a wash cycle. Without her children around to distract her, she'd managed to get the kitchen fairly well cleaned up and had made a casserole that was now bubbling away in the oven.

"Why is it so quiet? I don't hear any of the kids," Gabe said as he entered the kitchen. He looked around, as though they could be hiding under the table or chairs.

"They're with my mom." Libby wiped down the granite countertop surrounding the sink, then tossed the used cloth into a small laundry bin she'd concealed in a lower cabinet. The movement gave her a few extra seconds to collect her thoughts.

"Oh." He paused just inside of the doorway. "Maybe I'll go back to work then."

She froze in place, blood pounding in her ears. Her husband didn't want to spend even one minute alone with her. She'd barely said a word, and he already wanted to leave. Was this really it?

"What's going on with you?" she blurted out.

"Nothing." His tone was defensive. "I just have a lot of work to do."

"Are you cheating on me?" Her voice sounded tinny to her, as though she were listening to herself from far away. This was what her marriage had come to – standing in her kitchen, accusing her husband of being unfaithful.

His head reeled back, and he stared at her in horror. "No. Of course not. Why would you think that?"

"Because you're rarely home, and when you are, you're either sniping at me or standoffish. It's pretty obvious that you'd rather be anywhere else than here with me." She pretended to straighten a row of glasses in the dish drainer behind her, letting her hair hide her face and the tears spilling down her cheeks.

"Libby. You're not being fair." He sighed, and she turned around.

"*I'm* not being fair?" She grabbed a Kleenex, then made herself look directly at him. Lifting her chin, she said, "You're hiding something from me, and I want to know what it is." His expression was stoic, and she pressed on. "Correction, I need to know why you've been ignoring me. I can't take this any longer, and I don't think I should have to."

"Lib ..." He shuffled his feet.

"No. If you don't want to be married to me any longer, I deserve to know." She leaned the small of her back against the counter for support, not taking her gaze off him.

He crossed the room and wrapped his arms around her, lightly touching her back with both hands. "I'm not cheating on you."

Libby stood there, unspeaking, her body as stiff as a board. It had been so long since he'd shown any sign of affection for her that she wanted to relax into his embrace, but he hadn't given her any reason to trust him. She had to know what was going on between them.

She looked up at him, her fingers pressed firmly against her legs, refusing to reciprocate his affection. "Why have you been so distant then?"

He sighed again and stepped back, releasing her. She didn't take her eyes off him.

"Okay. You really want to know the truth?" He scanned her face, even as his own contorted with uncertainty.

"Yes! Of course I want to know the truth." She held her

breath. Was this the end of her marriage? A sense of calm came over her. Whatever happened, she'd take things one step at a time. She had the support of her family and friends. No matter what, she and the kids would be okay.

In a small voice, he said, "My company has filed for bankruptcy. I'm probably going to lose my job soon."

Her eyes widened. Gabe had worked at the same medical supply company for over six years, and as far as she knew, there had never been any hint of a financial problem before. In fact, it had only been a few years ago that they'd had a record year, and Gabe had received a big promotion and raise. "What happened?"

He shrugged. "Sales are down, and expenses are up. They're restructuring some of their debt, but I don't know if they'll survive." He reached behind him, gripping the counter until his knuckles turned white. "I'm sorry, honey."

"You're sorry?" She stared at him. "Why are you sorry? It's not your fault."

He hung his head. "I've been working so hard these last few months to get as many sales as I can, but even with doubling my efforts, it hasn't been enough. I didn't want to tell you how bad things were because I felt like I'd let you and the kids down."

The enormousness of the situation hit her. Gabe hadn't been ignoring her or thinking about a divorce. He'd been trying to save his company and his job. But why hadn't he confided in her before?

She moved closer to him, reaching out to touch his arm. "You've done everything you could do. It'll be okay."

He bit his lip. "We don't have the savings to weather me being out of work. With your mom being so sick last year and the catering business not bringing in much money, we've depended on the income from my job." He hurriedly added, "Not that I blame your mom. I know she needed the time off to recover. It's just that it's all hitting us at the same time."

Libby nodded. "I know." Her mind was spinning, calculating what they needed to survive. Raising four kids wasn't cheap. They had their mortgage, utilities, groceries, and a myriad of other expenses to take into account. Although the thought of Gabe losing his job was terrifying, part of her was relieved that he'd been avoiding her because of shame, not because he was cheating on her. *This* news, she could handle. She took a deep breath.

"This isn't something you needed to shoulder all by yourself. I'm your wife, your partner. You need to share things like this with me. I'll talk to Mom and see if we can take on additional catering contracts. And I'm sure you'll find a new position. It just might take some time. We'll figure it out – together." She moved forward until she was standing directly in front of him, and put her hands on his shoulders, turning her face up to peer into his eyes. "I love you."

A look of relief came over him and he bent down to kiss her on the lips. "I love you too." He put his hands around her waist and pulled her close, whispering into her hair, "Thank you."

With her cheek pressed up against his chest, she couldn't see his face, but from the raggedness to his voice and the way his arms trembled as they tightened around her, she knew she wasn't the only one crying. Her husband had tried so hard to hold everything together for their family, not wanting to burden her. Now, it was time for them to share that load.

Her muscles relaxed as she melted into him. Whatever the future brought them, they'd work through it as a team.

19

Zoe

Zoe regarded her to-do list with a critical eye. She'd never have believed it two weeks ago, but they were actually on track to complete all essential items by the end of July. It was a good thing, too, because they were now fully booked for weddings every Friday, Saturday, and Sunday in August.

The roofers would be gone by that afternoon, taking their massive garbage dumpsters with them – and, with any luck, leaving behind a beautiful new roof. Shawn planned to start renovating the guest rooms as soon as they left. For now, they'd just be hosting weddings on the lawn in front of the gazebo and down on the beach. Later, they'd offer overnight accommodations, but there was no way to have the Inn's interior ready by August.

She walked across the grass to the gazebo and climbed the steps, admiring the sheen of the new white paint as she peered into it. Shawn and his assistant had outdone themselves with the structure, even down to the smallest details, like the smooth curves on the backs of the benches inside. It was every bit as enchanting as the original building, but now she could stand in it without fear that she'd fall through a rotten floorboard to the ground below. In a few weeks, newlyweds would be standing on these steps, ready to begin their lives together.

The old Inn at Willa Bay had undergone its own renaissance of sorts, gaining new life as a wedding venue in modern-day Willa Bay. Thanks to Danville Hall's abrupt closure, the Inn had been inundated with requests for wedding dates, being in the unique position of not yet having any events booked for the rest of the summer. Every wedding vendor in town had pitched in to help those affected, and Zoe was glad that her new venue would be open in time to assist as many of them as they could. Even better, Zoe had snagged the Hall's staff florist and string quartet to bring on at the Inn before they could find employment elsewhere.

Zoe left the gazebo and continued walking around the grounds. Today was special, because for the first time, Luke was bringing Pops to Willa Bay to visit. Pops no longer drove, so in all the years she'd lived here, she'd always gone home to Haven Shores and Candle Beach to visit them. Finally, Pops would be able to see where she'd lived for the past decade – and, most exciting of all, see everything she, Shawn, and Meg had accomplished.

It would also be the first time Luke had been back to Willa Bay since he'd agreed to invest in the Inn. Anxiety nibbled at her stomach, but she pushed it away. She knew Luke had faith in her ability to make the Inn a successful venture, despite the times she'd doubted herself. Now, though, everything was coming together.

"Hey," Shawn called out from where he was taking a

break on the back porch. He got up and strode across the lawn to her. When he reached her, he leaned down to sweetly kiss her lips, sending pleasant tingles down her spine. He gently caressed her arm. "Are you excited about seeing Luke and your grandfather?"

She grinned. "I am. I can't wait to show them everything we've done."

"Me too," Shawn said. "I have to admit, I'm a little nervous about Luke visiting, like we're showing a term project to our teacher." He chuckled, but his words rang with truth.

Zoe hugged him, looking up into his eyes. "He's going to love it. You have nothing to worry about." She left one arm around his waist, but pivoted to scan the property. "Is Meg here? I wanted her to meet Pops too."

"She's around here somewhere. When we finished moving the table and chairs back into the kitchen, she said she wanted to spend some time in the old barn." Shawn lifted his hand to shield his eyes from the sun and peered in the direction of the barn. "I think she's getting antsy about remodeling it."

Zoe laughed. "Well, it's not going to be anytime soon. We've still got work to do on the main building." She knew Meg felt a little adrift, and Zoe hoped they'd be able to get to the restaurant portion of their master plan sooner than expected.

"Yeah, Meg knows that," Shawn said. "She just wants to use this time to let some of her ideas for a restaurant gel a bit."

Zoe nodded. "I get that. Sometimes I feel bad that we're all working so hard to make my dreams for the Inn come true, and she has to wait for hers."

He turned to face her and planted a kiss on the top of her head. "It will all come in time." He glanced at his watch, and then at the men walking around on top of the Inn. "And speaking of time, I need to check in with the roofers. I'm going to be so glad when that's finally finished."

"Me too," Zoe said. "I'll come find you when my family arrives, okay?"

"Sounds good." He took off toward the side of the building where the roofing company had piled their supplies.

Zoe turned back to her list, prioritizing the remaining tasks. Out of the corner of her eye, she caught sight of a woman in a turquoise tank top and jeans walking around the corner of the porch. "Tia? What are you doing here?" Tia wasn't scheduled to work that day, and an appearance from her on her day off couldn't be good.

Tia got closer and stopped in front of Zoe, her face drawn. "I'm afraid I have some bad news."

Zoe's heart skipped a beat. She should have known things were too good to be true. "What is it?"

"Apparently, the string quartet we hired for most of the August weddings accidentally double-booked themselves."

"You're joking, right?" Zoe's eyes drilled into the other woman. "How is that even possible? And why didn't they call me?"

Tia sighed. "They tried calling you, but they said you didn't answer."

"What?" Zoe fumbled in her pocket for her phone, but it wasn't there. "Shoot. The battery was almost dead this morning, so I plugged it into the charger. With Luke and Pops coming, I totally forgot to grab it." It hit her that she might have missed a call from them as well, and she started walking briskly toward the Inn's back door.

Tia followed close on her heels. "So, what are we

going to do about the string quartet? It was a big selling point for some of our clients."

Zoe frowned. "I don't know. Let me think about it." She opened the back door and stepped into the utility room where she'd plugged in her phone. The red message indicator on the phone blinked furiously, and she groaned. "I can't believe I forgot my phone." She unlocked the phone to check her messages. Six missed calls – two from Luke, and four from numbers she didn't recognize.

She quickly listened to the two voicemails from unknown callers. The leader of the musicians had called to explain the mix-up, and the other had been a call from someone trying to sell her something she didn't want. Luke had left a message telling her they'd be in Willa Bay around one o'clock, which meant they'd be there any minute.

Zoe looked at Tia. "I guess one of the musicians accepted a booking in Portland for the entire month of August and forgot to tell the others until now."

"Don't we have a contract with them?" Tia asked.

"Yeah, but I don't think it'll help much." Zoe stared out at the trees from the small window in the utility room. "The Portland gig is full time, so I don't think we're going to get them back. We can't realistically sue them, and I don't want to sever our relationship with them either. We're new to the wedding business, and we can't afford to cut off potential vendors. Besides, he was really apologetic about it."

"So, what now?" Tia leaned against the wall. "I guess we could use pre-recorded music for the ceremony. Most of our clients have already hired a DJ for the reception."

"Ugh." The idea of using canned music for the ceremony made Zoe's blood curdle. She wanted the Inn at Willa Bay to be known as a premiere wedding venue, and the string quartet had added an elegant touch to their ceremony packages.

"Oh!" Tia exclaimed. "I have an idea. My brother played in a musical ensemble while he was in college. It's summer, so maybe we could see if one of the local colleges has a lead on one for us."

Zoe regarded Tia. Her assistance had proven to be invaluable over the last few weeks. Her problem-solving skills and can-do attitude had come in handy as they helped potential clients navigate their cancelled contracts with Danville Hall, and assisted them in moving their dream wedding to the Inn. At times like this, Zoe had a hard time remembering why she'd objected to Tia in the first place.

"That's a fantastic idea," Zoe said. "Can you make the calls when you come in tomorrow?" If it didn't work out, Zoe wasn't sure what they were going to do, but she'd cross that bridge when they came to it.

Tia nodded vigorously. "I'll do it now. I don't want to lose out on finding replacement musicians because we waited an extra day."

Zoe shrugged. "If you don't mind, that would be great."

"No problem." Tia was already surfing the Internet to locate contact information for the local colleges.

From the other end of the house, someone knocked on the door.

"That's probably my brother," Zoe said. "I'll check in with you later. Thanks again for coming to the rescue."

Tia grinned widely. "No problem."

Zoe walked down the hallway to the front door, swinging it open. The first face she saw belonged to Pops, and happiness washed over her.

"Hi, sweetie," he said, opening his arms.

"I'm so glad to see you." She stepped forward into his embrace. Unexpectedly, tears filled her eyes.

"Are you okay?" he asked.

"Uh-huh." She sniffled and wiped her face with the back of her hand. "I just can't believe you're actually here."

"Hey, what am I? Chopped liver?" Luke joked from behind Pops.

Zoe reached past to hook her brother into their hug. "Nope, I'm happy to see you too." She looked past him. "Is Charlotte with you?"

"No, she really wanted to see you and all of the renovations, but something came up at the gallery, and she couldn't make it. She told me to take a lot of pictures of the Inn though." Luke held up his phone and made a point to turn around to take a photo of the gazebo.

Zoe laughed. "Well, there's plenty to document. I feel like we've already redone at least half of the property."

"I can tell." Luke gestured to the porch. "It looks brand new."

"Thanks." Zoe hugged him again, then turned to Pops. "Do you want to come in for a few minutes first, or do you want to see everything?"

"That was a long ride, and I had too many cups of coffee this morning," Pops said. "Can you point me in the direction of the men's room?"

"Straight down the hall and to the left," she said.

He nodded and disappeared through the front door.

Luke and Zoe stood on the porch together, gazing out at the bay. "I can't believe you've pulled this off," he said.

"Hey." She slugged his arm. "I thought you said you believed in me."

"I do. But this transformation is nothing short of amazing," he said. "I can't believe the three of you have accomplished so much in so little time."

A warm glow washed over Zoe. Luke's praise meant the world to her. "Thank you." She impulsively hugged him again.

"I'm ready to see the rest of the resort," Pops said as he neared the front door. "With all you've told me about the place, I feel like I already know it."

Zoe grinned. "I'm so excited to show it to you in person. I don't think anything I could say could do it justice."

She showed them around the resort, and they were properly impressed. Seeing the Inn through their eyes gave her even more of an appreciation for the history of the old building, and the resort as a whole.

They were coming back up the stairs from the beach when a truck's engine started up. The roofers were finally leaving, and a huge item could be checked off her to-do list. Tia waved frantically at her from the porch, and Zoe jogged over to her.

"What's up?" Zoe paused with her hands on her hips, catching her breath.

"I have the best news." Tia wore a huge smile on her face. "I located a string quartet for the August weddings."

"Really?" Zoe's eyes widened. "Where did you find them?"

"One of the local colleges came through. Apparently, they're really good, but they don't play many gigs in the summertime. They're excited to have the chance to play here." Tia handed her a piece of paper with the contact info for the musicians. "I told them they might need to audition first, and they said they were happy to do so."

Zoe looked around the grounds. The renovations hadn't all gone as planned, but everything had still come together because she had a team that she could trust. "Nope. If you've vetted them, I'm good with hiring them."

Tia's eyes lit up. "I'll let them know." She turned and went inside, dialing her phone as she walked away.

While Zoe was talking with Tia, Pops and Luke caught up to her.

Luke raised his eyebrows at Zoe. "You let someone else manage a big decision for a wedding?" He shook his head. "Now I've heard it all. My sister, the control freak, is learning to be part of a team."

"Hey," she laughed. "I resemble that remark."

Pops gave her a hug. "Sweetie, I'm so proud of you. This place is wonderful, and I can't wait to see it in full swing. Your grandma and parents would have been proud too."

She swallowed a lump in her throat. "Thanks, Pops. That means a lot to me." Her parents had died when she was only a toddler, and her grandparents had raised her and Luke.

She pulled both Pops and Luke in for a big group hug. "Thank you both for everything."

"Ah, sweetie," Pops said, tears glistening in his eyes. "We love you."

Luke squeezed her shoulder, "Love you, sis."

Zoe dried her own tears and smiled at Pops. "Now, let's go find Shawn, Meg, and Celia. I want to introduce you to some of the other important people in my life."

She took a deep breath and surveyed the resort, admiring the gazebo that was a symbol for the Inn at Willa Bay's rebirth. All of her life, she'd sought approval from Pops and Luke. While she still loved them and valued their input, making the resort come alive again had given her a sense of purpose that had renewed her own faith in herself.

It didn't matter how many roadblocks they'd encountered in renovating the property, she and her trusted team had conquered everything. When they officially opened in ten days, she had no doubt that the Inn would quickly become the most sought-after wedding destination in the Pacific Northwest. Everything she'd worked for her entire life was finally coming together.

20

Kyle

Kyle tucked the tails of his blue button-down shirt into his khaki pants and checked out his appearance in the mirror. He'd never been to the grand opening of a bakery before, so he might be a little overdressed, but he wanted to make a good impression on Cassie. This was it – the day that he'd tell her he still had feelings for her.

Based on what she'd said in the pizza parlor about wanting her independence, he may very well walk away from the bakery with his heart crushed, but he had to try. If there was any chance of getting Cassie back, he didn't want to lose it.

He winced at his reflection. His face was pale, an outward display of the butterflies in his stomach. He was more nervous now than he'd been on the day he'd asked her to marry him. At least on that day, he'd had a pretty good idea that she'd say yes.

It was now or never. He straightened his collar, squared his shoulders, and walked out the door. When he arrived, the bakery was overflowing with customers. Some patrons relaxed around the outside patio tables, and even more were inside, chatting with friends or standing in line to order.

The bakery was only open for a few hours this afternoon, in preparation for a full day tomorrow. Cassie had told him she was getting together later with the Wedding Crashers, her group of friends in the event industry, but Kyle hoped he'd have enough time to whisk her away for a surprise after the bakery closed.

Cassie stood behind the register, wearing a blue dress and white apron, her face glowing as she rang up purchases. Amanda waited next to her, ready to fill their orders. Nearby, Jace folded cheery yellow boxes and stacked them in front of his sister.

Kyle's heart swelled with pride as he stood back, watching them. His family was operating like a well-oiled machine. Only he was missing from the picture. With a flash of guilt, he wondered if he should have offered his assistance. However, he soon realized that Cassie's friends, Meg, Libby, and Zoe, were helping out as well. Even Celia had a part and was stationed near the door, greeting customers with a warm smile.

Cassie saw him leaning against the wall and beamed at him. He smiled and waved back at her.

"She's doing great, isn't she?" Zoe said. With all the crowds, he hadn't noticed her approach.

"She is," he said softly. He couldn't take his eyes off Cassie. She looked so happy and excited, something he hadn't seen in a long time. With all of the stress from the kids, she'd needed something like this in her life, something that was hers alone.

"You care about Cassie, don't you?" Zoe asked.

He pulled his attention away from his ex-wife and

turned to look at Zoe. He paused, wanting to choose his words carefully. "I do care about her. A lot."

Zoe peered into his eyes, then hesitated. "I don't know if I should say anything to you about it, but I think she still has feelings for you."

He stopped breathing for a moment, not sure if he'd heard her correctly. "She does?"

Zoe narrowed her eyes. "Yes. And judging by the way you can't stop looking at her, you feel the same way about her."

He took a deep breath. "I do." His words fell out of his mouth in a jumble. "I've tried to move on, but I can't. She's the only woman I want to be with."

Zoe nodded, then broke out into a smile. "Good." She poked her index finger into his chest. "But if you ever hurt her again, you'll answer to me. Got it?"

He glanced down at her finger, then met her gaze. "I'd never hurt her." He looked over at Cassie and the kids. "Would you be willing to do me a favor? I have something planned for Cassie after the bakery closes. Could you watch the kids for us for an hour or two?"

"I'd be happy to," Zoe said. "I can take them back to the Inn with me. We can always use more laborers." She winked at him. "Seriously, though, Celia and I will get them something for dinner, if that's all right with you. We'll bring them along with us to the Wedding Crashers meeting, and you can pick them up there. How does that sound?"

"That's perfect. Thank you so much." He cast another glance at Cassie. "I hope this works."

"Me too." Zoe smiled and lightly touched his arm. "Cassie deserves to be happy."

"I know." He checked his watch. "I'm going to finish

getting things ready for my surprise. Could you let Cassie know I'll pick her up after the bakery closes?"

"Sure." Zoe eyed him. "I can't wait to hear more about this surprise from Cassie later."

"I'm sure you will. With any luck, you'll hear good things, not bad." His stomach churned with nerves. So much was riding on the next few hours.

"Just be yourself and listen to her. That's all Cassie wants." She gave him a little wave, then disappeared into the back room.

Kyle peeked at Cassie, but she was immersed in her work, smiling broadly the whole time. He gazed at her for a moment, memorizing her look of joy. He hoped his surprise would make her just as happy. He waved to Jace and Amanda, then wove his way to the door through the groups of townsfolk.

When Kyle returned to the bakery, the crowds had dispersed, and the sign on the door had been flipped to Closed. He knocked on the door, and Amanda unlocked it for him.

"Hey, Dad," she said. "Zoe said you were going to take Mom somewhere, so Jace and I get to see what they've done at the old Inn." She peered at him. "Where are you going with Mom, anyway?"

He paused, not sure how much to tell his daughter. If things between him and Cassie didn't work out, he didn't want to get her hopes up. "I just want to take her out to celebrate," he said finally. "She's been working hard, and she deserves some fun."

"Hmm." Amanda eyed him. "Okay. But next time, I want to come with you."

He grinned. "Next time, we'll all do something together." At least, he hoped they would. If his plan backfired, he could accidentally ruin the peace that he and Cassie had worked so hard to attain. Was he doing the right thing in telling Cassie how he felt?

Amanda turned away from him, heading back to the table where she'd set her backpack and schoolwork, and Kyle walked toward the back of the bakery. He stopped in the doorway. Cassie was standing near the ovens, talking with Zoe. Her expression was serious, and he wondered how much Zoe had told her about their conversation.

Zoe caught sight of him and waved. "Hey, Kyle. I'll just grab the kids, so the two of you can get out of here." She scurried out of the room.

Cassie smoothed the skirt of the cornflower blue dress that matched her eyes. "Am I dressed okay for wherever we're going?"

He nodded, his throat thickening. "You're perfect." Heat rose up from his collar, but he didn't try to correct his statement. She *was* perfect, and he wanted her to know that.

Her cheeks turned rosy, and she hung her head shyly. "I don't know about that."

He wanted to take her in his arms right then, but he was afraid he'd scare her if he did. Instead, he asked, "Are you ready to go?"

She looked around, biting her lower lip. "I think so. Let me get my purse."

When they got out to the main room, Zoe had already left with the kids. Cassie locked up, then stood with him outside on the sidewalk. "Where are we going?"

"It's a surprise." He winked at her.

She tilted her head to the side. "I don't know if I'm up for a surprise. It's been a long day."

"Oh, I think you'll like this one," he said. "But I'll give you a hint – we're going down to the waterfront."

"Okay. I'm up for that." She smiled up at him. "Thanks for taking me out to celebrate. I've been so caught up in the grand opening that I've barely had a chance to eat or breathe today, much less celebrate." She skipped for a few steps, which he found endearing. "I can't believe how successful today was. It seemed like everyone in town was there."

"I wouldn't doubt it. When Edgar left, everyone was worried about who would take his place, but I think you've shown them that they had nothing to worry about."

"I did, didn't I?" She turned her face up to the sky, and grinned. "I couldn't have asked for a better grand opening." Her stomach grumbled, and she laughed. "I'm really hoping this celebration of yours involves food, or you're going to need to grab me a burger on the way back to town."

They crossed Willa Bay Drive and walked along the pedestrian pathway through the woods, emerging at the parking lot. "Is that your car there?" She pointed at his blue sedan.

"It is." He took a chance and reached for her hand. She hesitated, then grasped it. He tugged gently on her fingers to lead her over to his car. "I have a few things to get out of here."

She squealed when he opened the trunk and revealed the old-fashioned wicker picnic basket he'd purchased at a thrift store for the occasion. "That's so cute. I've always wanted one of those."

"I know." He swallowed hard. Cassie loved picnics, and he should have taken her on more when they were married. It was one of the little things that could have made all the difference in their relationship.

He grabbed the handles of the basket and a large outdoor blanket, then shut the trunk lid. "C'mon." He started walking back the way they'd come, into the woods.

Cassie eyed him with confusion. "I thought we were having a picnic on the lawn."

"Nope." He continued on, not stopping until they'd reached a rugged trail leading off from the main path.

Her eyes lit up. "You remembered!"

"Of course I did." He smiled, remembering all the good times they'd had together as teenagers. Up ahead, the river burbled loudly as it spilled over the rocks, and a small clearing appeared. Just enough brush shielded the clearing from the prying eyes of anyone boating on the river, but still allowed for a peek-a-boo view of the water.

When they neared the riverbank, he spread out the blanket and opened the picnic basket. She helped him pull out summer sausage, cheese, crackers, and grapes, then sat down on the blanket.

"This looks so good. I can't believe how starved I am." She grabbed a few grapes and popped them into her mouth. "Did you bring anything to drink?"

From under the cloth napkins at the bottom of the basket, he retrieved two bottles of strawberry wine cooler.

She laughed. "I can't believe you brought that. I used to think I was so cool drinking these, but I haven't had one in years." He removed the cap from one bottle and handed it to her, turning his body to face her. She took a huge swig, then made a face. "It's a lot sweeter than I remember." She held it out to him to try.

He took a sip and grimaced. "No kidding. I think our tastes have changed a lot since then."

"We've both changed a lot," she said quietly.

"I know." He moved closer to her on the blanket until

their knees were almost touching and searched her face. "Cassie, I need to tell you something."

Her eyes met his. "Okay."

He stretched his hand out to cover hers, and she turned hers to press her palm into his. Every nerve in his body tingled as the sensitive skin on the pads of their fingers touched.

"I'm in love with you. I think I always have been." He sighed. "I know the divorce was all my fault. I took you and the kids for granted and wasn't there for you."

She shook her head. "No. It wasn't just you. There were two of us in the marriage, and I should have communicated better with you. I should have fought harder for us." Her voice cracked. "I'm still in love with you too. I tried so hard not to be, but I can't help it." She laughed a little. "I think we may be stuck with each other."

He caressed her soft cheek. "I can't think of anyone I'd rather be stuck with."

Tears formed in her eyes and she leaned closer to him, her lips meeting his. As soon as they came together, it was like seeing the Fourth of July fireworks all over again. This was how a kiss was supposed to be. He pulled her onto his lap and wrapped his arms around her, deepening their kiss.

She leaned into him hungrily, her fingers weaving sweetly through the hair on the nape of his neck. It may have been because they'd been separated for so long, but this was even better than he'd remembered it. He ran his fingers up and down her back.

Behind them, a branch crackled, and they reluctantly broke apart.

"What was that?" Cassie asked breathily.

"I don't know." Kyle was about to get up from the

blanket when a cottontail rabbit poked his head out of the bushes and merrily hopped through the clearing.

They looked at each other and broke out into laughter.

"I thought for sure my parents were going to catch us kissing again," Cassie joked.

"Me too." He grinned at the long-ago memory.

She sobered. "Do you really think this will work? Us, I mean?"

He sighed. "There isn't anything I want more in this world. I'm not letting you slip out of my grasp again."

She glanced at the sickly-sweet wine coolers. "We're not the same people anymore."

"No." He cupped the back of her head and kissed her forehead, then released her. "We're not." He reached into the picnic basket and took out a bottle of Cristal. "But that doesn't mean we're not right for each other." He uncorked the champagne and poured it into two plastic flutes, handing her one. "This time though, we have to grow together, not apart."

She nodded. "I'd like that." She held out her cup and tapped it against his, the hard plastic clicking as it connected. "To us – growing old together."

They both took a drink. This time, she smiled. "I think we're definitely more like Champagne people now."

They both laughed, and he snaked an arm around her waist, drawing her close as they sipped their bubbly and gazed out toward the river channel. Being with Cassie made him whole again, and he fully intended to do everything in his power to keep his promises to her.

21

Cassie

Cassie was floating on air as she and Kyle walked back to the Sea Star Bakery, holding hands with their fingers intertwined. Electricity and anticipation sizzled between them with every step, and for the first time in years, her world made sense. The bakery's grand opening had been a huge success, she was about to hang out with her closest friends, and, best of all, she and Kyle were back together.

Something was bothering her, though. As they neared the bakery, her footsteps grew heavier and she tugged lightly on Kyle's hand.

He stopped, and turned to face her. "Is everything okay? You haven't changed your mind, right?" His eyes widened as he waited for her response.

She grinned. "No, I definitely haven't changed my mind." She stood on her tiptoes and gave him a peck on the lips, then cast a glance at the bakery's front door. "It's just that the kids are in there and I don't know what to tell them."

He nodded. "Because if things don't work out, we don't want them to be hurt." He caressed her cheek. "I get that and it's fine to not tell them. But – this time – things will work between us. This time, we're going to make sure we communicate better and are there for each other, even when times are tough."

She looked at the bakery again. "Yeah, that's part of it. I don't want to get their hopes up if things sour between us – not that I think they will." She put her hand on his chest and kissed him again before looking deeply into his eyes. "I want to take it slow, so we can work through things without being flung into the deep end all at once." She sighed. "And, selfishly, I want our relationship to be just us for a while, something that the kids don't factor into."

He raised his eyebrows. "Uh ..."

She laughed. "Yeah, I know. We'll still do family stuff together. I only meant that we could go out on dates together without the pressure of them knowing that we're getting back together. I want us to have time to get to know each other again – as individuals, not just as co-parents."

"Like a secret relationship?" He squinted into the sun and then a smile spread over his face. "I think I like it. It'll be like we're in a romantic spy movie or something. Is it okay to tell other people, though? You'll still tell your friends, right?"

"Of course I'm going to tell them." She chuckled. "I'm sure Zoe is going to grill me about it as soon as I walk in the door."

"Okay then." He squeezed her hand. "Now, we'd better get you to your Wedding Crashers meeting. I've got a full evening of junk food and movies planned for the kids."

She peered at him. "Not too much junk food, right?"

He gave her an innocent look. "Of course not."

She laughed and pressed close to him. It felt wonderful to joke with Kyle, just like they used to do.

They went around to the back of the bakery and Cassie slipped inside. Zoe had unlocked the door using a key Cassie had given her, and judging by the noise level, most of the Wedding Crashers were already present.

"Hey," Cassie said as she walked into the main room. Her friends had arranged several smaller tables in a group and everyone was crowded around them, drinking coffee or wine as they chatted. Amanda was sitting with the women, while Jace hung out at a table in the corner by himself, happily playing on his tablet, his ears covered by headphones.

The women looked up.

"Hey, Cass." Zoe pushed her chair back and stood. She peered past Cassie with a worried expression. "Where's Kyle?"

"He's waiting out back for the kids." Cassie's lips twitched, knowing Zoe could barely contain herself from asking if she and Kyle were back together.

"Oh," Zoe said carefully. "Did the two of you have fun?"

"Uh-huh." A warmth spread across Cassie's face at the thought of their romantic picnic by the river.

Zoe nodded knowingly. "Good, I'm glad."

Cassie went over to Jace and removed his headphones. "Hey, buddy, it's time to go to Dad's apartment."

"Okay." He stood, not taking his eyes off of his tablet, and walked blindly toward the back room. The other women must have told Amanda that Kyle was waiting, because she'd grabbed her little purse and was disappearing down the hall. Cassie followed them to make sure they found Kyle.

At the door, Kyle laid his hand on Jace's shoulder to

guide him outside. He locked eyes with Cassie, making her breath catch. "I'll talk to you tomorrow, okay?"

She nodded. "Okay."

When the kids were headed away from the bakery, he turned and waved at her, mouthing the words, "I love you."

"I love you too," she mouthed back, watching the loves of her life as they disappeared around the corner. She leaned against the doorframe, filled with happiness. In time, her family would be back together, the way they were meant to be.

Cassie re-entered the main room of the bakery and took a seat next to Zoe. Celia, Tia, Meg, Libby, and Debbie were seated around the other tables across from them. Samantha, Debbie's youngest daughter after Libby and Meg, hadn't arrived yet.

"So?" Meg asked. "Are you and Kyle back together?" She popped a potato chip in her mouth as she waited for Cassie's response.

Cassie mock-glared at Zoe. "I see someone can't keep their mouth shut."

Zoe shrugged, then grinned at Cassie. "Sorry?"

"Like you weren't going to tell us anyway." Libby took a sip of white wine, then looked at Cassie expectantly. "So? Are you back together?"

"Yes," Cassie said, unable to stop the huge smile that overtook her whole face. Even her eyes felt like they were smiling. Everyone cheered at her announcement. "But don't tell the kids," Cassie warned them. "We don't want them to know yet."

Debbie nodded approvingly. "Makes sense. You can make sure everything goes well without worrying about them."

"I'm so happy for you," Zoe squealed, wrapping her

arms around Cassie. "I think things are going to work this time around."

"Me too." A wave of joy rushed over Cassie. She grinned at her friends. "Now, what else is new?"

"Well, we have our first wedding next weekend at the Inn." Zoe smiled, but Cassie noticed her friend had a death grip on the stem of her wine glass.

Cassie patted Zoe's arm. "It'll be beautiful. Make sure you take some pictures."

Next to Zoe, Celia nodded vigorously. "I'm planning on it, if Zoe doesn't." She beamed. "This is so exciting. You have your bakery now and Zoe is managing the premiere wedding venue in the area."

"No kidding," Tia said. "The phones have hardly stopped ringing with potential clients lately. My schedule is packed with appointments for showings."

"I knew I was smart to hire you." Zoe grinned at her.

"Right ..." Tia drawled. Cassie was happy to see her exchange a friendly glance with Zoe. They seemed to have worked through their issues from when Tia started out at the Inn.

"Hey, where's Samantha?" Cassie asked. "Is she coming tonight?"

Libby shrugged. "I have no clue. I called to tell her about the meeting, but she never responded." She turned to Debbie. "Have you heard from Sam at all?"

Debbie shook her head. "No. Not for a few days. She's been really distant lately." She frowned. "I don't know what's going on with that girl."

"I'm sure she's just busy. I saw her around town yesterday." Meg bit into a bear claw and washed it down with a slug of coffee. "But come to think of it, I haven't talked to her in over a week either."

"I'll call her tomorrow," Debbie said. "You girls know I get worried when I don't hear from you for a while."

"Yes, Mom." Meg made a face. "You know we're all adults, right?"

Debbie narrowed her eyes at Meg. "And you remember that I'll always be your mother, right?"

Libby elbowed Meg. "Give up. You're not going to win this one."

Meg grinned, but said nothing.

"When do you think you'll start on the restaurant?" Libby asked Meg.

Meg looked over at Zoe. "In a few months?"

Zoe nodded. "Probably. It depends on how long it takes to finish renovating the Inn. We need to get the guest rooms completed before we start on another project."

Meg pressed her lips together tightly and got up from the table, bending over to pick up the coffee carafe. "I'm going to make another pot of coffee." She walked behind the counter and fiddled with the coffee maker.

"Is Meg upset that the restaurant won't be ready any time soon?" Cassie whispered to Zoe.

"A little." Zoe grimaced. "I feel bad about it, but there's not much I can do."

"Can you start clearing out the barn?" Debbie asked. "Meg mentioned that it's packed with junk. That might help get her out of this funk she's been in." She looked worriedly at Meg, who's back was still turned to them.

"I can help," Libby said. "I'd love to see what all was stored in the barn over the years."

Celia laughed. "I'm afraid it contains a little bit of everything. I don't even know what all is in there." She sobered. "But, it would be nice to get started on it. Maybe there will even be some old furnishing or décor from back in the day. That would be nice to see."

Meg came back to the table and set the carafe on the table with a loud thunk. "What would be nice to see?"

"Oh, the Inn, once it's finished." Celia smiled serenely at her. "Now, let's get down to gossip. I feel like I'm out of the loop. Have any of you heard why Bruce Danville really left town?"

Cassie watched as her friends chatted amongst themselves, interjecting her own observations as warranted. She sat back in her chair, sipping a cup of hot coffee and relaxing. It had been a long day, but if she ever had the chance to relive any day over and over again, this would definitely be it. Her kids had been a wonderful help at the bakery's grand opening, as had her friends. And that picnic with Kyle – she couldn't have asked for anything better. Yes, today was a day to treasure.

She looked over at the mural wall to her left. A soft ray of light reflected off a metal napkin dispenser, illuminating the image of the man and woman sitting on the bench overlooking the Pacific Ocean. It was almost like Sofia Valencia was smiling down on the bakery, happy to see so much love and laughter in the room. Cassie let her gaze soften as she stared at the couple in the painting. Originally, the mural's subject had made her ache with memories of the past. Now, it was a beacon of light and hope for everything the future would bring. One thing was for sure – she knew exactly where she and Kyle would be spending their second honeymoon.

EPILOGUE

Meg

"Less than a week until we open." Zoe surveyed the exterior of the Inn and then fixed her attention on Meg, who was standing next to her. "Are you as nervous as I am?"

Meg grinned. Zoe was doing enough worrying for both of them. "Maybe not as much as you, but I am a little." She shaded her face with her hand to take a closer look at the Inn. Sun gleamed off of the new windows, their white trim freshly painted. A soft breeze swept through the flowers bordering the front porch, scenting the air with their fragrance. Across the lawn, the gazebo stood tall, waiting to shepherd couples into marriage. "I never thought I'd say this, but I think we're ready for the first wedding on Saturday."

Zoe took a deep breath, then smiled. "You're right."

Meg gave her a quick hug. "I know I am. Everything you've done here is paying off." She gently turned her friend around to face the Inn's front door. "Now, I think a special someone is waiting to take you to dinner." She waved at Shawn, who was standing on the porch, gazing at Zoe with a bouquet of yellow roses clutched in his hands.

Zoe's face lit up when she caught sight of the roses. She shook her head slightly and whispered, "How did I get so lucky? The resort, Shawn, all of this."

"It's not luck." Meg rested her hand on Zoe's shoulder to reassure her. "You've worked hard all your life and you're one of the most amazing people I know. You deserve all of the goodness life can give you."

Zoe bit her lip and nodded. "Thank you." She smiled. "You always seem to know what to say."

"Well, at least I've got that going for me." At the moment, the rest of her life wasn't too stellar, but at least she could be there for her friend.

Zoe hugged her tightly, whispering in her ear. "It'll be your turn soon."

Meg scoffed, but her stomach tightened. If only it were that easy. "Get up there and accept those flowers from him."

Zoe laughed, and waved at Meg before jogging up the stairs, directly into Shawn's arms.

As he pulled Zoe into a tight embrace, the knot in Meg's stomach constricted further. Zoe was so happy, and Cassie and Kyle had reunited. Even Libby seemed happier these days. But where did that leave Meg?

She walked away, her feet taking her in the direction of the old barn behind the Inn, as if on autopilot. Once upon a time, it had stabled up to eight horses, offering guests a chance to ride on the beach or one of the other trails in existence at the time. Now, it was used only for storage.

She lifted her head, noting the broken and missing

glass in some of the window frames. The barn had once been bright red, but the paint had long ago cracked and faded away, exposing the battered gray of the wood below. The surrounding lawns had been manicured to the same exacting detail as the rest of the grounds, but longer grass licked at the barn's foundation.

She tugged on the handle of the side door, scraping aside small rocks and dirt as she opened it. Inside, sun shone through the missing windowpanes, catching dust motes dancing through the air. Beds and dressers had been pushed into horse stalls and miscellaneous machinery covered huge swaths of the main aisle. Cleaning out the barn would be a huge undertaking, one she wasn't looking forward to.

Meg picked her way around a farm tractor to reach the ladder to the hayloft. Although Shawn had done a thorough inspection of the barn and pronounced both the main structure and its interior to be safe, she tested the first rung of the ladder by stepping on it and bouncing a little. It creaked, but held her weight.

She climbed to the top, moving about a foot away from the ledge to sit cross-legged on the floor. The loft was strewn with straw and remnants of twine from decades-old hay bales, but hadn't been filled to capacity with junk like the main floor of the barn. Looking out over the edge, she was struck by the sheer size of the building. The barn didn't look that big from the outside, but from here, she could fully imagine it as a restaurant – her restaurant.

She intended to paint the interior and exterior walls white to achieve a clean, yet rustic appearance. The kitchen would be located under the hayloft, but most of the main floor would serve as a dining room, with the capacity to host large wedding receptions. She pushed herself up, stifling a sneeze as she brushed hay off her jeans. After visually assessing the floorboards for stability, she made her way over to the large window at the end of the loft.

Most of the panes were covered with so much dirt that she couldn't see out of them, but the broken sections offered her a chance to check out the view. As she'd hoped, there was a clear line of sight to Willa Bay. The upper level would be perfect for romantic sunset dinners.

What would it be like when the restaurant opened? She closed her eyes, imagining waiters bustling around, the clatter of a busy kitchen, and the low murmur of patrons chatting and enjoying her food. She smiled at the vision, her spirits lifting.

The pocket of her lightweight jacket vibrated as her phone rang, and she reluctantly pulled herself back to the present. Theo's number popped up on the screen, and she glanced at the phone's clock. More time had passed by while she was lost in her daydream than she'd realized.

She answered. "Hey, hold on a moment." She scrambled down the ladder. "Sorry about that, I was up in the barn's hayloft."

"No worries," he said. "Are we still on for dinner tonight?"

"I'm so sorry. I lost track of time. I'll be there in ten minutes, okay?" She leaned against the barn's open side door, waiting for his response.

"Sure. Sounds good. I'll see you soon."

"See you." She ended the call and stuffed the phone back into her pocket, taking one last look inside. Like a Cinderella story, the whitewashed walls of her restaurant had turned back into a rundown barn.

Her excitement faded as she shut the door tightly behind her. Realistically, with all the projects planned for the Inn at Willa Bay, they wouldn't start remodeling the barn for at least three months. Whether she liked it or not, her life was in a holding pattern.

At least she had Theo. That was the one bright spot of her current situation. They'd been dating for a little over a month and had intentionally kept their relationship light. Cassie and Zoe seemed so happy in their serious relationships, though. At thirty-two, was she supposed to want something more? She shook her head. For now, she was having fun – something she'd sorely missed over the last two years.

Meg stopped in the middle of the lawn separating the Inn from the barn and looked back. She closed her eyes once more and her restaurant came alive again, with twinkling fairy lights hanging whimsically from the barn's white eaves. She opened her eyes, and smiled. Someday, hopefully soon, her dream would become a reality.

Author's Note

Thank you for reading The Sea Star Bakery! If you're able to, please consider leaving a review for it.

Wondering what's in store for Meg? Find out what happens next with Book 3, A Haven on the Bay.

If you haven't read Willa Bay's sister series, the Candle Beach Novels, check out Book 1, Sweet Beginnings.

Happy reading!

Nicole

ACKNOWLEDGMENTS

Thank you to everyone who's helped me with this book, including:

Editors: LaVerne Clark, Devon Steele

Cover Design: Elizabeth Mackey Design